HAL

RIDING HARD
BOOK 8

JENNIFER ASHLEY

JA / AG PUBLISHING

CHAPTER ONE

Lucy Malory glanced up from her keyboard in the tiny but bright reception area of Riverbend's veterinary clinic to see the town vet, Dr. Anna, cell phone in hand, beaming at her.

"What's up?" Lucy asked.

Anna leaned a hip on Lucy's desk. The young blonde woman was trim as ever, except for her very round stomach that indicated she'd soon be having Lucy's brother's kid. These days, Anna was high on pregnancy and found everything joyful.

"Ranch needs help with a calving," Anna said, as though she'd announced someone was having a huge party in her honor. "Want to come?"

"Sure," Lucy said without hesitation.

Lucy's job as Anna's veterinary assistant was mostly bookkeeping and paperwork, but Lucy enjoyed the opportunity to interact with the animals. She'd proved adept at holding a dog or cat calm while Anna injected various meds or examined eyes, ears, and mouth.

The livestock was interesting too—Lucy hadn't realized how much she'd missed being around horses and even cattle during her years away in a pristine Houston-based condo.

Lucy shut down her files and caught up Anna's bag full of large animal vet accoutrements. Anna was amused at Lucy for insisting on carrying all the heavy totes these days, but Lucy wasn't about to let Kyle's wife get hurt. Not only would Kyle be devastated, but Lucy had come to love Anna as well.

Anna seemed especially chipper today. She trotted out to her truck, arriving well before Lucy, and had the pickup running when Lucy climbed in. Anna gunned the engine before Lucy could even latch her seatbelt, the truck's tires spinning in the mud. The Hill Country had seen an unusual spate of rain this March and muddy puddles were everywhere.

"What's going on?" Lucy adjusted her seatbelt and eyed her sister-in-law. Anna plowed through a puddle, laughing at the water spraying over the hood. "You going into labor, or something?"

"No, not yet." Anna was due in early April, and both Kyle and Lucy watched her cautiously. Anna was healthy, though. *Like a really healthy horse*, she'd tell them.

"Then what?" Lucy asked. Anna's overly cheery mood was sending up red flags. "You're acting weird."

"Am I?" Anna said, too brightly.

"Yes." Lucy skewered Anna with a sharp gaze. "Where exactly are we going?"

"The Kennedy Ranch." Anna spoke the words innocently.

Lucy stared at Anna in dismay, then she groaned. "I should have figured."

Hal Jenkins was the manager of the Kennedy Ranch.

"If I'd told you, you wouldn't have come," Anna said. "And I really need your help."

"Seriously underhanded, Anna."

Anna sent Lucy a sideways glance. "You can't hide from him forever."

"Sure, I can." Lucy forced a smile. "It's easy. I go to work, I go home—everything's fine."

Lucy's home these days was the small house in the center of town where Anna used to live. A cute, cozy abode that Lucy had started fixing up with her own decor. Walking distance to shopping or places to meet friends—not that Lucy had been doing much socializing. This job and a comfortable space to rest her head was all she needed these days.

Anna didn't answer, but her silence spoke volumes. Everything wasn't fine. Lucy's entire life had changed more than a year ago when she'd walked out on her job, her boyfriend, and her rapidly advancing career.

Well, she hadn't had much choice with the job and boyfriend. She'd assumed that Clyde would become her fiancé, until Clyde had announced his engagement in front of the entire company—to someone else. Then he'd fired Lucy.

Looking back, Lucy wondered what she'd ever seen in the asshole. Hal Jenkins would never pretend to be in love with her while all the time secretly planning to marry another woman. Hal would never gaze condescendingly at Lucy and say, "What we had was fun, but ..."

Hal would never say a mean word to anyone. He was kind-hearted, spoke in a low but friendly voice, and the corners of his eyes crinkled even if a smile didn't move his mouth. He was a big man who could make frenzied bulls in the ring suddenly tuck in their tails and run for the chute. At the same time, he was as gentle as summer rain.

Hal was a better man than Clyde, a hundred times over.

His eyes when he spoke to Lucy—when he could bring himself to look at her—were warm and brown ...

The truck listed as Anna took a corner, and Lucy snapped herself out of her reverie. Damn it, why was she always thinking about Hal? There was nothing there. Or at least, if there was something, it was going nowhere fast.

"Cheer up," Anna said. "Maybe Hal won't be around today. It's a big ranch. He might be in the back section working on whatever."

Yes, that would be better, wouldn't it? If Hal wasn't there at all? Much easier, Lucy thought morosely. Right?

Damn it.

———

HAL WAITED ON THE GRAVEL DRIVE IN FRONT OF THE Kennedy ranch's office trailer and tried to quit checking the horizon for the dust that would announce Dr. Anna's arrival. Anna hadn't said she'd bring Lucy along, but these days, as Anna was ready to pop with her son or daughter, she usually did.

Hal vowed he wouldn't choke this time when he saw Lucy. He'd say in easy tones, "Hey, Luce, how are things going?" Then he'd enjoy the sound of her voice as Lucy outlined her plans to return to stockbroking in some far-off place, maybe Los Angeles or a big city back east.

Lucy had never out-and-out said she was leaving, but she'd hinted at it whenever they'd spoken. She'd shaken the dust of Riverbend from her feet before, and she'd do it again.

Hal wished he could be easy with women like the Campbell and Malory brothers or his friend Jack. After Lucy and Anna finished up today with the calving, Hal could walk Lucy to the truck, open the door for her and say, "Hey, baby, how about we go out this weekend?"

Hal's face heated. He couldn't ever imagine the words *Hey, baby* coming out of his mouth.

He also didn't want to watch Lucy look everywhere but at him while she thought up an excuse not to go. He sure needed to figure a way out of this stalemate between them before he did something crazy like blurt out to Lucy exactly how he felt about her.

Hal's phone pealed, thankfully tearing him from his thoughts. He slid the cell out of his pocket and studied the screen, lit up with a number he didn't recognize. That wasn't unusual—Kennedy's ranch did business with people all over the country. Or it might be a telemarketing call, but Hal still answered, to be polite.

"Hey, this is Hal Jenkins."

"Jenkins. How are you?"

The male voice was hearty and strangely familiar. Hal frowned in puzzlement a moment, before cold stole through him.

Couldn't be. That was over with—Hal was done.

"Don't hang up," the voice said. "I want to talk to you."

"Well, I don't want to talk to you." Hal wrenched the phone from his ear, thumb hovering over the red button to end the call.

"You're going to want to hear me out." Nate Redfern's arrogant tones floated up from the speaker.

Hal lifted the phone to his mouth again. "The hell I will. If I see you anywhere near me, I'm going to kick your ass so hard you'll never sit down the rest of your life."

"You'd like to think so, but I have things to say you might want to listen to."

"Seriously?" Hal's body tightened like it hadn't in years. His jaw began to ache, and his neck muscles grew rigid. "I told you, I'm finished with you and your crew. You don't want to mess with me."

"I'm not messing with you. I'm in town. Yes, your Podunk shit town you're trying so hard to hide in. I know all about your perfect new life and your cute new girlfriend ..."

Hal clenched the phone so hard he feared the plastic would break. "You stay the fuck away from—"

Redfern's laughter sounded then cut off as he ended the call.

Hal lifted his head, barely able to see through the red rage that misted his eyes. He'd hoped Redfern would be in prison for many years to come—he'd even heard the rumor that Redfern had died inside. The man had pissed off enough people that plenty wanted him six feet underground. But no, Redfern was alive and trying to wedge his way back into Hal's life.

And he knew about Lucy.

As Hal glared at the hilly horizon, he spied the plume of dust he'd so eagerly searched for before the call.

At the front of the plume was Anna Lawler-Malory's small pickup, minus her shoeing trailer today. He couldn't tell if there were one or two people in the cab, but his throat closed, and his heart banged until he was queasy. If Redfern came anywhere near Lucy, Hal would ...

Hal wasn't certain what he would do. Best thing if Redfern never saw her at all.

Shit.

Hal thrust the phone into his pocket, stretching the hand that had cramped around it. He set his mouth in a firm line and strode grimly forward to meet the truck.

CHAPTER TWO

Lucy climbed slowly from the pickup Anna parked in front of the ranch office and tried not to let her gaze fix on Hal, who waited for them.

Nope, she wouldn't notice his muscular form that filled out his button-down work shirt and jeans, his hard but handsome face, his thick hair cut short, the dark strands dusty. Hal's body was strong from riding, ranching, and wrangling. So very strong.

Just be cool, Lucy told herself. *We see each other at the bar and the diner. Hal's a friend, just a friend ...who happens to be a roasting-hot kisser...*

Lucy abruptly cut off the memory. No need to fixate on the knee-weakening kiss Hal had given her the day her brother Ray and his wife had opened their B&B. Since then, Lucy and Hal had spoken together on occasion but nothing more.

At Christmas, Hal had joined Lucy and family at the B&B. She'd sat across from Hal at the table but hadn't been able to find any intimate moments with him. The conversation that day had been loud and animated, Hal eating his dinner and listening to the Malory family go on and on. And on.

After New Year's, things had become busy for Anna and Lucy at the vet's office as well as for Hal and the other ranchers. Animals required care every day, no matter the weather or what was going on in the humans' personal lives.

Anna had parked so that the pickup was between Lucy and Hal as Lucy slid from it, which was a blessing. It gave Lucy time to straighten her shirt, brush her pants free of dust, and make sure her hair looked okay. She glanced into the big side mirror on the truck's door and surreptitiously wiped a bead of sweat from her nose.

Lucy cleared her throat, slung the bag with Anna's equipment over her shoulder, and strolled nonchalantly around the back of the pickup. Anna was already talking with Hal about the cow they were going to assist.

Hal glanced up at Lucy. His gaze landed on her and stayed there, which surprised her. No avoiding looking straight into her eyes, no coming up with an excuse to turn away or focus on something else.

Lucy held on to her courage. "Morning, Hal." She strove for a light and breezy tone, one friend greeting another. "How are things?"

Hal continued to stare, an anger behind his gaze that Lucy had never seen before. The mouth that had kissed her with such promise was pressed into a grim line, no humor in his eyes.

Lucy's lips parted, hurt touching her heart. She drew a breath to make some joke about him being rude—Hal, of all people—but he snapped his head around to Anna, shutting out Lucy completely.

"She's this way," Hal said curtly. He strode toward the barn, splashes of mud spattering in his wake.

Lucy's jaw slackened with surprise. What the hell just happened?

Had she been reading too much into Hal's shy conversations and the impulsive kiss? Maybe he was tired of her sliding onto the barstool next to him at Sam's Bar and going on about her life in Houston. Or tired of her coercing him to Christmas dinners with her family. Or something.

Anna lingered to give Lucy's arm a reassuring pat. "Hal's worried about the cow."

Her words were forced—Anna was trying to make excuses for him.

The cold truth was that Hal had just given Lucy the brush-off. Lucy's throat tightened but she lifted her chin and smiled shakily at Anna.

Anna looked relieved that Lucy didn't argue, and she hurried after Hal's retreating figure. Anna would switch all her attention to the birthing cow and push Lucy's troubles to the back of her mind until later. As Lucy should. They were here to do a job.

The cow had been isolated in a large corral near the hay barn. The corral was big enough not to confine the animal too closely but small enough to keep her from charging around and getting hurt. Right now, the cow lay on her chest, her wide brown eyes fixed on a point beyond the corral's bars, clearly wondering what was going on at her back end.

"You remember Molly," Hal said, his voice gruff and matter-of-fact. "Usually, she pushes her calves out pretty quick, but she started straining and groaning, yet nothing's coming."

"Stuck in the pipe somewhere," Anna said cheerfully. She

always began optimistically with animals, declaring that if she believed she could help them, the odds went up that she could. "Let's have a look."

Hal had worked with vets in this type of situation before and had prepped the area with a tarp so Anna could stretch out on the ground. He'd also provided a plastic bucket of warm water and the antiseptic soap Anna liked. He led Anna to this without looking once at Lucy. It was as though she'd dropped off the face of the planet. Lucy pretended not to care, but her throat ached.

Anna washed her hands, slipped on gloves, stretched out on the tarp, and proceeded to slide her slim arm into Molly's birth canal. The poor cow never flinched.

Anna and Lucy had visited this particular animal before when she'd cut herself brushing against a barbed wire fence. On that day, Hal had warned Anna that Molly was unfriendly and never gentle, but Anna, being Anna, had only patted the cow's side and plunged her needle of local anesthetic into Molly's shoulder. Molly had sighed and let Anna scratch her between the ears before Anna had cleaned and sewed up the wound. Anna had the touch.

Lucy knelt at the edge of the tarp, ready to hand Anna whatever she asked for. Anna hummed a little tune as she felt around for the trapped calf, and Molly visibly relaxed.

"There he is," Anna said in delight. "Nothing serious, I don't think. One of his legs is bent wrong. Here we go." She closed her eyes and concentrated on whatever she was doing to get the calf unstuck.

Lucy was happy that Anna wasn't asking for the large forceps or heavy-duty painkillers, or worse, the dose that would put both cow and calf out of their misery.

Anna alternately spoke coaxingly to Molly or continued

humming, while Hal stood a few feet away, hands on his hips as he watched Anna.

"I wonder if Anna will be this chipper when she's having her own baby." Lucy forced herself to send Hal a teasing grin. "Or if she'll prefer a tarp in a corral to a hospital bed."

"Anyone would," Anna answered, her forehead against the cow's hip.

Hal switched his gaze briefly to Lucy. Instead of the flicker of amusement she expected, that endearing crinkle at the corners of his eyes, he remained cold. The chill of his stare burned her like an unexpected brush of frost.

Hal moved his attention back to Anna and the cow, again shutting Lucy out.

Damn it. Lucy blinked, lifting her gloved knuckle to quickly rub the corner of her eye. She could blame the hay scattered on the ground, even though she wasn't allergic, or the smell of cow, which she was used to by now. She was definitely not crying because Hal Jenkins didn't like her anymore.

They didn't have a relationship, she scolded herself. They barely had a passing friendship. Lucy couldn't lose what she didn't have, could she?

So why did she want to burst into tears and flee like an upset teenager?

Hal's just a friend of the family's. A ranch manager Anna and I sometimes work with. Nothing more.

The voice behind this one, the one that told Lucy the truth about herself, said that she hadn't felt hurt like this since Clyde stood up at the company office party and announced he was marrying the pretty woman at his side.

Lucy remembered how the floor had dropped out from under her feet, how she'd barely been able to see let alone paste on a smile and join in the applause. She didn't know to this day how she'd made it from the party to her apartment before she lost her shit.

This isn't the same, she tried to tell herself. Clyde had been her lover for years, had taken her on expensive vacations, rented her a luxury apartment. His kept woman, she'd realized.

In contrast, she and Hal had shared a few beers and one great kiss last year. Their conversations had remained friendly and neutral. That was all.

So why did she feel like someone had just kicked her in the chest?

"Lu." Anna's commanding tone jolted Lucy out of her speculations.

Diminutive Anna could snap out orders like a drill sergeant, and Lucy and Hal obeyed her like good soldiers. Lucy handed Anna instruments, and Hal helped reposition Molly's hindquarters at Anna's instructions.

"It's coming," Anna sang. She was having the best time of anyone.

Two tiny feet protruded from Molly's birth canal, followed by the hint of a nose. Anna dropped her instruments with a clatter and reached for the calf.

"Grab a hoof!" she yelled to Hal.

Hal obediently knelt beside her and grasped one of the small hooves, his big hands competent and gentle. Lucy gathered up the tools Anna had scattered to keep them out of the way of the emerging calf.

Molly, wanting to get on with things, gave a mighty heave. The calf tumbled out, surrounded by its birthing sac. The slimy, glistening, writhing creature landed right in Hal's lap.

Lucy burst out laughing. The mucus-covered calf squirmed and kicked, sending Hal onto his back, the calf on top of him. Molly struggled to her feet, the cord still connecting her with her offspring. Anna was ready with a scalpel, if needed, but the cow's sudden desire to rise broke the cord and released the afterbirth ... which also landed on Hal.

Any other cowboy, Lucy's brothers included, would have cursed and snarled and scrambled away in disgust.

Hal, on the other hand, kept hold of the calf, swiftly clearing its nose so it could draw its first breath. His wonderment as he gazed at the calf made him look like his normal self again.

"Welcome, little guy," Hal said, in a voice so tender that Lucy's eyes moistened once more.

The calf gulped air and then let out a loud *Maaaaaa!* Molly turned in place, lowered her head, and began to lick.

"Little *girl*," Anna corrected Hal. "A heifer. A pretty one."

Molly's tongue revealed a white spot on the calf's wide head between its now blinking eyes. The baby calf remained on Hal's lap, Hal covered in blood and goo, while the cow licked and licked.

Anna unfolded to her feet. She joined Lucy in regarding the maternal tableau of cow, calf, and Hal caught beneath them.

"That's a picture," Anna said.

Lucy grabbed her phone from her back pocket and snapped a photo. "I'm printing it to put up in Sam's bar."

"Aw, come on," Hal said, but good-naturedly.

His coldness had vanished, and his lips twitched as the cow nearly knocked him on his back with her enthusiastic calf-bathing.

The calf struggled to get its legs underneath it. Lucy was happy to see that the extra time wedged in the birth canal hadn't hurt it. No sorrow today. In fact, the calf was energetic and strong. Soon, it was wobbling on shaky legs, moving to seek its mother's milk.

Molly kept licking but when the calf found its breakfast, she let out a satisfied *moo*. Molly then glared at Lucy, Anna, and Hal, as though wondering why they were intruding on her precious moment.

Lucy slid her phone into her pocket and extended her hands in surgical gloves to Hal to help him up.

"It's okay, I'm protected," she joked.

Hal's cool demeanor returned like a slap. He ignored Lucy's offer of assistance and hauled himself upright, a frown replacing the hint of a smile he'd worn while holding the calf.

"Guess I better get showered," he said to Anna.

Anna waved a hand in front of her face and wrinkled her nose. "You'd be put on a no-fly list if you showed up at an airport like that. Declared a danger to society."

Hal's eyes briefly held amusement. "Thanks for your help, Dr. Anna. Send the invoice to the office."

"No problem." Anna stripped off her gloves and washed up in the bucket, then lifted it to find somewhere safe to dump the water.

Hal jumped for the bucket. "I got that."

Anna backed away. "Eww. No. Don't come near me. You might send me into labor."

Hal's alarm at her statement was comical. Lucy wavered between mirth and hurt at Hal completely closing himself off once more.

"That's what I'm for." Lucy reached for the heavy bucket. "Keeping Anna whole and healthy. Though she could probably kick both our butts with one hand tied behind her."

Hal switched his frown to Lucy, as though he couldn't understand why Lucy was attempting to be funny. Aloof politeness settled over him, and he gave them a collective nod before turning and marching out of the corral.

Lucy watched as Hal headed past the office toward the trailer where ranch hands stayed when they worked overnight. Water sloshed from the bucket she held onto her boots, but Lucy barely noticed.

Anna joined Lucy as Hal reached the trailer, yanked the door open, and disappeared inside without looking back.

"He's had a hard morning," Anna said in a quiet voice. "Tough when you think you might lose an animal."

"Don't try to make me feel better," Lucy answered. "I'm fine. Like the saying goes, maybe he's just not that into me."

She hoped to sound cheerful, but tears blurred her view of the house, Anna, and the now-happy cow and her incredibly adorable calf.

Lucy made herself blink away the tears, hauled the bucket to an open space behind the mare pens, and vented her feelings by dashing the contents onto the dust and grass. The water flowed out in a rush, to be swallowed by the grateful earth.

———

Lucy spent a restless night, alternately telling herself she was imagining Hal's frosty reception and wondering what she'd done to piss him off.

The next morning, Lucy forced herself out of the warm bed, and dressed in jeans and a cute top to meet her brother for their traditional breakfast at Riverbend's diner. Anna always allowed herself the luxury of a long sleep-in on Saturdays—though she remained on call for emergencies—and Kyle and

Lucy had begun the habit of meeting over coffee and eggs to catch up.

Lucy's house was only a few blocks from the diner, so she headed out the door, ready to walk there.

Her next-door neighbor, Mrs. Kaye, was in her garden, watering the petunias she'd planted as soon as the weather had warmed enough for flowers. Lucy caught the scent of growing things and upturned earth on the breeze.

"Morning, Mrs. Kaye," Lucy called, and waved.

"Morning, Lucy," Mrs. Kaye answered cheerfully. "I saw that nice Hal Jenkins at the hardware store yesterday. Now, when are you two going to get married?"

CHAPTER THREE

L ucy stopped herself from stumbling down the steps, the morning's beauty marred by Mrs. Kaye's question.

"Uh. She frantically tried to come up with an answer. "I don't think there's any question of me marrying anyone, Mrs. Kaye."

Mrs. Kaye regarded Lucy in surprise. "You and Hal are right for each other. It's plain to everyone in town."

Lucy let out a breathless laugh. "Is it? We barely know each other. We haven't even had a real date."

"That doesn't matter," Mrs. Kaye said with confidence. "It will happen." She set down her watering can. "Want to make a bet?"

Lucy blinked. "I'm sorry? What?"

Mrs. Kaye rummaged in her jacket pocket, pulling out a small notebook and a tiny pencil. "Let's see, I'll give you better odds because you can influence the outcome. How much do you want to wager?"

"Nothing at all," Lucy spluttered. "I—"

"I'll put you down for twenty dollars to start." Mrs.

Kaye's pencil scratched in the notebook. "If you want to increase the bet as things progress, you can, but your odds will be worse."

Lucy could only stare at her. "Mrs. Kaye, what are you talking about?"

Mrs. Kaye made a final notation and returned the notebook to her pocket. "I'm the usual bookie for any interesting wagers in this town. What gender Anna's baby will be, who will win the competitions at the Fall Festival, whether Hal and Lucy will get together. We're pretty sure Ms. Marvin and Jack will, but will they make it stick?"

Lucy's surprise turned to irritation. "You can't bet on other people's lives."

"Why not? I'm old and bored. Or do you believe that anyone over sixty-five should just move into the nursing home and wait?"

"No, of course I don't think that ..."

"Those of my generation aren't a collective gray-haired crowd with walkers," Mrs. Kaye went on with indignation. "We are still very much alive, thank you, with our own interests, problems, relationships, and lives. We used to be you." She pointed a steady finger at Lucy, then her voice gentled. "Life goes fast, Lucy. Treasure it while you can. Treasure *him.*"

Mrs. Kaye's eyes grew moist. She and her husband had been madly in love until the day he'd died. Everyone knew that.

"I'm sorry." Lucy wasn't certain quite what she was apologizing for but said it anyway. "Sure, put me down for twenty. Against. It's probably not going to happen."

Mrs. Kaye had the notebook out so fast again her movements blurred. "All right, but you'll lose." She beamed at Lucy.

"You have a good day, now. Meeting your brother for breakfast?"

All of Riverbend knew each other's business.

"Yes. What are you doing today?"

Mrs. Kaye's expression turned shrewd. She was well aware she'd guilted Lucy into being interested in her activities.

"Finishing the flowers, then joining Dena for our martial arts class."

Dena was the head librarian at River County's library. "Oh." Lucy peered at Mrs. Kaye to see if she was joking, but the woman's mouth remained straight, her gaze unflinching. "Well. Have fun."

"It is fun," Mrs. Kaye said. "Say hello to Kyle for me. He'll be a daddy soon. Hard to believe it." She chuckled, as though she knew exactly how much Kyle was panicking about that.

Mrs. Kaye lifted her watering can and turned away, signaling she was finished talking to Lucy. Lucy went on down the steps, dazed by the entire encounter.

She continued on foot for the few blocks to the town square and the diner. Mrs. Ward had owned and operated this diner for as long as Lucy could remember, keeping the town from sticking to any kind of weight-loss plan. The most determined dieter melted when confronted with Mrs. Ward's mouth-watering pies. Though in recent years, Mrs. Ward had conceded to make a few of them sugar-free and others gluten-free.

The diner was full this Saturday morning, with many Riverbenders digging into mountains of pancakes, scrambled eggs, or biscuits and gravy. Lucy smiled at Mrs. Ward's hurried welcome as the lady raced by with an armload of plates. She slid into a booth across from Kyle, who was downing a large cup of black coffee.

Lucy, a regular, didn't need to tell anyone her order. Any moment now, a latte with a dollop of whipped cream and cinnamon sprinkles would land in front of her.

"I just had the weirdest conversation with Mrs. Kaye," Lucy said after she and Kyle had exchanged easy greetings. "She told me she was taking a martial arts class. Do you think that's true? Or was she B.S.ing me to see how gullible I am?"

Kyle lifted his coffee mug. "Nope, she's learning jujitsu. She and Dena. Olivia Campbell set it up at the community center. You can take jujitsu, karate, and judo. If you want something a little slower, there are classes for tai chi and yoga."

"Huh." Lucy gave a young waitress, one of Mrs. Ward's granddaughters, a grateful nod as her latte arrived. She sipped, savoring the bitter coffee through the sweet cream and cinnamon. "I guess I've had my head buried at the office. Vets are busy around here, as you know."

"I am aware, yes." Kyle gave her an amused nod.

"I hear the Campbell boys want their mom and Sam Ferrell to have a big wedding this summer," Lucy said, groping for topics beyond her own troubles. Olivia Campbell and Sam Farrell had become a couple at Christmas.

Kyle laughed. "They would." The Campbells and the Malorys had a long history of feuding, though they'd buried that now as Campbells married into the Malory family. "They should let them find their own way. Like we do with Mom and Miles."

"That's because Mom told us right off the bat to keep out of her business," Lucy reminded him. Miles Dunham was a software engineer in Austin, and their mother lived happily there with him. They hadn't married—yet—and fended off all questions about it. Lucy understood. She'd acquired her ambition to have her own life and do her own thing from her mother.

"A lot of complicated relationships start in this town," Kyle concluded.

"Speaking of complicated—" Lucy broke off as their food was delivered. Kyle's eyes brightened at the stack of pancakes and side of bacon sliding in front of him, and Lucy eagerly lifted her fork for the eggs Benedict.

"Speaking of complicated—" Kyle prompted after the waitress departed and they'd taken a few bites.

Lucy sighed. "You know Hal pretty well. Is anything going on with him?"

Kyle's dark brows instantly snapped together over green eyes that had prompted girls all Lucy's life to use her to get close to Kyle. "Why?" he demanded. "Is Hal messing with you?"

"No." Both Lucy's brothers continued to be annoyingly protective. "He hasn't done anything. I've barely spoken to him since Christmas. I was wondering if he was upset about something, that's all. Anna and I went out to the Kennedy ranch yesterday to help with a calving, and he—" Lucy made patterns with her fork in her hollandaise sauce. "He just wasn't himself."

"Not himself?" Kyle's frown relaxed. "Who was he then?"

"Don't make fun. He was acting strange. Cold and angry." She tightened with the memory. "Like he was sorry to see me there with Anna."

Kyle's expression changed once more to concern.

"You're right, that isn't like Hal." Kyle sat back, lifting his coffee cup to his lips. After a swallow he said, "In all the time I've known him, he's always been super polite, even when he's worried."

"He wasn't speaking at all if he could help it. He's usually quiet, but this was weird."

"Hmm." Kyle took another sip of coffee, set down his cup, and returned to his pancakes.

"That's it?" Lucy demanded. "Just *hmm*?"

Kyle swallowed a mouthful. "I can't read the guy's mind. Especially when he's not even here. Maybe he got some bad news."

"From where? I don't know much about Hal, really," Lucy admitted. "He told me once his parents were enjoying retirement traveling the world, but I don't know where his home is. Our conversations haven't gone there."

Kyle contemplated his pancakes for a moment. "I'm not sure either. He's been on the rodeo circuit forever, which is where I met him a long time ago. Won a boatload of belts. One time in Lawton, he—"

Lucy quickly held up her hand to cut him off. Kyle could go on about a rider's stats for a good hour if he wasn't stopped.

"I'm more interested in his life on the ground. Why did Hal stop riding?" Lucy returned to her plate—Mrs. Ward's eggs Benedict were not something to waste.

"He told me he'd taken one too many bad falls" Kyle said around forkfuls. "Though I never saw any of those. I mostly saw him win. When he did fall, he knew how to not hurt himself. But one day a few years ago, he turned up here in the ring as a rodeo clown because he'd decided he'd rather help keep both riders and bulls safe."

That sounded like Hal. He was always helping people. That made his behavior yesterday all the more strange.

"Do you know if he was married? Or at least had a long-term relationship in the past?" An ex coming out of the blue could upset a person.

"No, he's never been married," Kyle said. "He told me that once. I don't know about other relationships. We didn't really get into that much detail. Have never seen him with a girl-friend, anyway."

Lucy silently acknowledged her relief at this information. She was not going to let herself fall for a guy who was attached to someone else. She didn't need that heartache again.

"And you don't know exactly where he's from?" Lucy asked.

Kyle shrugged. "Texas."

"Funny. Could you narrow that down?"

Texas, a state larger than many countries of the world, had several distinct regions. A person was usually careful to distinguish from which part they hailed. East and West Texas were very different places with very different climates, and South Texas deserts were a world apart from the Red River area of North Texas.

"His accent says West," Kyle concluded. "I think he lived out in San Angelo for a while. Or maybe it was closer to Midland. Somewhere in West Texas, anyway. But that's still a big place. Is what town he's from important?"

"I'm trying to figure out what happened to piss him off at Anna and me." Lucy slid a piece of her English muffin through the remains of the sauce. "If it was bad news from home, we might have friends from wherever his family lives who would know what was going on."

"You're not going to spy on him through his hometown friends," Kyle said in disapproval. "Gossip is bad enough here without you spreading it all over the state."

"You're a lot of help. Do you have any better ideas?"

"I have one." Kyle lifted his fork again with determination. "Ask him."

Lucy heaved a withering sigh. "You are such a guy."

"I figure it's his business. Or maybe you did do something." Kyle narrowed his eyes. "Are you seeing someone else?"

Lucy blinked in surprise. "Someone else? When do I have time to see anyone at all? I work all day, have maybe one drink at the bar with whoever is there, and go home. By myself."

Kyle shoveled the remaining bits of pancakes into his mouth. "Who've you been talking to at the bar?"

"Christina, when she has time to drop by. Bailey, sometimes. Mostly Rosa, who is there because she works there, and Karen, same. I have a lot of conversations with Karen."

Kyle pretended to shudder. "Don't start acting like Karen, all right? Please. I'm begging you."

Karen Marvin, who owned and managed the bar, as well as other ventures in town, could be a tough-as-nails business-woman who took no shit from anyone. Lucy had to admire her. Karen also liked dating good-looking cowboys ten years younger than herself, though lately she'd been seen around with Jack Hillman, who was a biker and one of the town's bad boys.

"Karen's cool," Lucy said. "I like her."

"I like her too. But I don't want her for my sister."

Lucy chuckled—it felt good to banter with Kyle. "The point is, I hang out with girlfriends at the bar. Rarely talk to a guy, unless it's you or Ray, or the Campbells, all of *them* happily married. There is a decided lack of single men in town these days."

"Not during rodeo season," Kyle pointed out. "Maybe Hal thinks he doesn't have a chance with you. Have you been flirting with him enough? Or only kissing on him?"

Lucy's cheeks went hot. "I kissed him *one* time. We were

caught up in the excitement at the B&B opening. And I don't flirt with him. I talk to him like a normal person."

"The trouble with *guys*, as you keep calling us, is we don't always get when a woman likes us." Kyle tapped the side of his head. "We can be dense. If we chase a woman, we're called a creepy stalker, so we wait for them to tell us they're interested. It's hard for us to know for certain if they don't walk up to us and say, *Hey, how about it?*"

"Sure, because Anna was sashaying her hips and sending you love notes. It took *forever* for you two to work it out."

"Exactly my point." Kyle's gaze went remote in remembrance. "I thought she was gorgeous but also that she hated me. You need to tell Hal you want to go out with him. He probably thinks you're biding your time to return to some big city, looking for another billionaire."

"Clyde wasn't a billionaire," Lucy said.

"No?" Kyle pretended to be amazed. "Maybe that was the problem. Aim higher next time, Lu."

"No." Lucy made a wiping motion with her hands. "No more privileged daddy's boys who think they can have whatever they want, no matter who gets hurt." Her fingers shook as she lowered her hands. "I'll stay in Riverbend for a while. Even if I go home alone every night."

It was lonely, but also restorative. One day, though, Lucy would be rested enough, and she'd have to decide what to do with her life.

For today, Lucy enjoyed her breakfast and bonding with Kyle. For the first time in her life, Lucy was truly connecting with her brothers and sister, and no matter her confusion over Hal, she wasn't in a hurry to give up the modicum of peace she'd found.

Hal spooked whenever his phone rang Saturday, but Nate Redfern didn't try to contact him again.

Business at the Kennedy ranch went on as usual. One of the women in Riverbend taught horseback riding on Saturday mornings, and Hal stayed to make sure the horses were taken care of and the kids didn't get hurt.

Three of the students were offspring of Campbells and Malorys: Faith Sullivan, Dominic Campbell, and Erica Malory. Erica was Lucy's niece—step-niece, Hal corrected himself. Ray had adopted Erica, just as Tyler Campbell had adopted his stepson, Dominic.

Faith, never timid, hailed Hal and walked up to him after she'd finished supervising younger children, who'd brushed down and returned the horses to their pens. Faith was now an assistant riding teacher, as she was already a champion in her age group.

Nearing thirteen, Faith was growing into a beauty. Her dad, Carter, would soon be terrifying Faith's would-be boyfriends. Hal felt a tickle of amusement. That would be fun to watch.

Not that Hal would let anyone less than perfect go near Faith. He was as protective of his friends' kids as their parents were.

"How's it going?" Faith asked, as Hal lifted bridles from the racks where the students had left them. "It looks like Katie might need a hoof trim. She was favoring her right fore, but I couldn't see anything wrong except a little bit too much hoof."

"I'll check it out," Hal said. "Thanks."

Faith remained motionless as Hal started to turn for the tack room, which was a shed attached to the end of the barn.

The riding ring was empty now, wind scattering dust over Hal's boots.

"So, Hal," Faith continued, waiting for him to turn back.

Hal did so, his brows rising in inquiry.

"The Bluebonnet Festival," Faith went on. "Three weeks from now. Are you coming? And are you bringing Lucy?"

CHAPTER FOUR

H al hid his sudden discomfiture by studying the bridles as though worried they were tangled.

The Bluebonnet Festival was a newish party Ray and Drew Malory had started at their B&B, the Bluebonnet Inn. The festival featured an afternoon picnic and barbecue, which later turned into a dance with a live band in a marquee erected behind the big house.

Erica glided to a stop behind Faith. The two girls, a year apart in age, had become best friends, and dressed similarly in jeans, T-shirts with the Circle C Ranch logo on them, and cowboy boots. Two pairs of eyes skewered Hal, one hazel, one blue, their demanding stares tougher than those of the hardest ranch hands Hal knew.

"Not sure," Hal rumbled into their intense focus. "Hadn't really thought about it."

"Well, you have to come," Faith said. "Everyone likes you, and they'll want to see you."

"And you have to bring Lucy," Erica put in.

Bits jingled as Hal fumbled with the bridles. "How do you figure?"

The stares became glares. "Because you like her," Faith declared.

Hal's face warmed. "Yeah, she's nice."

Erica rolled her eyes. "*Nice?* She's wonderful. Just ask her, okay? She needs to quit moping around and have some fun."

"She's totally over her bad breakup," Faith went on. "And you're way better than the dude she was with."

"Way better," Erica seconded. "My dad and Kyle call him a name I'm not allowed to say. Even Grace calls him that. Once Lucy's with you, she'll forget all about him."

Hal privately agreed that Lucy was better off without the asshole, even if he had no idea how to form a response. He wondered if things had been so clear cut when he'd been thirteen. Probably not. Girls usually figured out life and how to fix it faster than boys did.

"She might not want to go with me," Hal ventured.

The girls uttered identical exasperated laughs. "Just ask her," Erica repeated.

"She'll say yes," Faith said with conviction. "See you there, Hal."

Satisfied that they'd achieved their purpose, the two pivoted and walked away, calling farewells over their shoulders.

Dominic Campbell, who was going on twelve, shuffled past, carrying a heavy Western saddle toward the tack room. "Girls," he said, with the confidence that Hal would know exactly what he meant. "They should mind their own business."

Hal's lips twitched. "I don't think they know how to."

"Huh. You got that right. They try to tell me what to do *all the time.*"

Hal followed Dominic into the tack room and hung the bridles on the hooks for those that needed cleaning. He helped Dominic dump the saddle onto a saddle tree, Dominic exhaling in relief once it was out of his arms.

Dominic was more comfortable dirt biking with his mom than horseback riding, which was very new to him. He enjoyed the horses, but Hal had the feeling he'd agreed to the lessons because horseback riding was Faith's favorite activity more than any real interest of his own.

"Women enjoy telling men what to do," Hal said companionably. "We pretend to go along with it to make them happy."

Dominic's scowl deepened. "Why don't they think about making *me* happy?"

"Oh, they will," Hal assured him. "You'll find a girlfriend someday who'll do anything for you. When you do, though, you'd best make sure not to be selfish and take all they're willing to give. They can end up hurt that way, and we don't want the ladies to be hurt."

Dominic thought about that. "No, we don't."

"So let them boss you," Hal said. "Then be grateful for the girl who does want to make you happy. And try to make *her* as happy as she can be. You'll have a good life that way."

Dominic ran a hand through his short hair then shrugged. "Okay. I'll try that. Are you going to do what they say and ask Lucy to the dance?"

"Mmm, not sure about that."

"Why not? Aunt Lucy does like you. Aunt Grace says so."

Hal's embarrassment returned with a bang. He hadn't realized his interest in Lucy was such a widespread subject of discussion.

"Well, I don't know," he managed to say. "Let's see how things work out, okay?"

"Okay." Dominic wiped his hands on the legs of his jeans. "See you, Hal."

"See you, Dominic. Say hi to your folks for me."

"Will do." With that, Dominic strode off. He was much easier to appease than the girls had been.

Hal had no intention of asking Lucy to the party—not until he was sure Redfern had been taken care of anyway. Keep the ladies happy, he'd told Dominic. That included keeping them safe. Hal would stay far from Lucy until Redfern was gone for good.

It wouldn't be easy. He'd barely held himself together yesterday when Lucy had come out with Anna for the calving. Her lively green eyes, her warm smile, her gentle teasing, had rooted him in place. He'd had to swiftly shut down his fantasies of being naked with her, touching, kissing, nipping....

Having a newborn calf plus its birthing bag fall on him had helped keep him grounded. Though watching Lucy laugh, her face lighting up in merriment, had been worth it. He'd cover himself in muck anytime if he could only see her smile.

The fantasies returned with wild intensity, spiking a need through Hal that would demand a cold shower to shut down.

Damn, this was going to be hard.

———

HAL SOMEHOW GOT THROUGH THE REST OF HIS WORKDAY and left for his small home on the outskirts of town, a red-brick house shaded by a stand of live oaks. There, he bathed and changed his muddy clothes, had a microwaved tamale dinner

as the sun sank, and then took himself into Riverbend to
Sam's Bar.

Sam's was where everyone in the county went on a
Saturday night. Hal could catch up with friends or watch the
dancing from a barstool while listening to the laughter. No one
ignored him, but no one bothered him either. Hal enjoyed the
simplicity of sitting among people who liked each other. No
crazy dramas, no danger. This was why Hal had moved to
Riverbend.

Lucy wasn't here tonight, he saw when he entered, which
was a good thing. Hal planted himself on his favorite barstool
and began to nurse the beer Rosa had dispensed for him.

A glance around showed him that Lucy hadn't actually
posted the photo of him covered with newborn calf mess as
she'd vowed to. Either she hadn't had time, or she'd decided to
be nice and not embarrass him.

Sweet of her.

Hal cut off the thought. He had to quit thinking about
Lucy. He needed to keep his distance from her, at least until
he could—

"Kind of boring in here."

Hal sensed Redfern's presence before he heard the hated
voice, and felt the man slam himself to the stool next to him.
Rosa approached cautiously. Her disapproving frown told Hal
she'd heard Redfern call the place dull.

Redfern winked at her. "A beer, sweetheart. Whatever's
on tap. Don't make it a light one if you want a tip."

Rosa, who had three teenage sons and was beyond intimi-
dation, thrust a mug under the tap and jerked it to splash out a
draft beer. Usually, she was careful with the foam and set a
nice head, but this time she simply banged the mug to the
counter, letting foam slosh over.

"Six-fifty," she announced.

"Seriously?" Redfern stared at her. "That's criminal. What did you charge *him*?" He jerked a thumb at Hal.

"Just pay it," Hal advised.

Redfern, aggrieved, dug out his wallet and took out a ten. "I'll be counting the change," he growled, as he dropped the bill onto the bar.

"No, she keeps the rest," Hal informed him. "For putting up with your shit."

Redfern regarded Hal disparagingly. The man hadn't changed much as far as Hal could see. Same beefy arms filling out a T-shirt that was pulled down to hide a slightly tubby belly. Same tufts of light brown hair sticking out from under a baseball cap, this one with an Astros logo. Light blue eyes regarded Hal from a round, somewhat sunburned face.

"If she keeps my change, I'm giving her even more shit," Redfern declared. He delivered this threat with a partial smile, which was how he usually gave his ultimatums. As though he knew no one would challenge him.

When he hadn't been challenged in the past, it was probably because he'd had four or five other big guys hanging around him, spoiling for a fight. Tonight, Redfern was alone— or at least it looked that way.

Hal had never been cowed by Redfern, which had started the bad blood between them in the first place. "If you don't give her the tip, you won't walk out of here with your knees straight."

Redfern continued to regard Hal with an obnoxiously amused expression. Redfern knew damn well Hal could hurt him if Hal chose, knew it from experience. Hal had the reputation of being a nice guy, but with Redfern, he made an exception. Redfern was a bully, had assaulted plenty of people in the past, and Hal had learned that the man would only keep civil if threatened.

Redfern must not be running with his buddies tonight, because he shrugged, pushed the ten at Rosa, and waved her away. Rosa accepted the cash and moved to the register, ignoring Redfern completely.

"This is swill anyway." Redfern made a face after he took a sip. "Seriously not worth the money. But I guess since this is the only place in town, you have to put up with its crap."

The bar's draft beers, brewed by a local company, were both full-bodied and refreshing. People drove for miles to drink them. Karen Marvin stocked only the best.

Hal decided not to argue with Redfern. Waste of breath.

"I heard you gave up the bull-riding life," Redfern said. "I always knew you were a chickenshit."

Hal let the insult flow past him. His reasons were his own, nothing to do with fear, and Redfern's words slid off his back. He shrugged, letting Redfern believe what he wanted. Hal didn't owe the dickhead any explanation.

"Why are you here?" Hal asked him. "Didn't you go to prison?"

Redfern sipped more beer, apparently over his dislike of the brew. "I'm sure you guessed why I'm here. We could do some good business in this town. Rodeos come through, so do cattle shows, and there's a big county fair in the fall. Plenty of opportunity to make a lot of money."

"No," Hal said immediately. "I'm out of all that. Best day of my life was the one when you and your friends got arrested."

"Which is why some of my boys wanted to kill you." The corners of Redfern's eyes crinkled as though he'd made a joke. "I argued with them that it hadn't been you who turned us in."

He regarded Hal intently, as though prompting Hal to confirm the statement.

"It wasn't," Hal answered. Not technically.

Hal had been on the verge of risking his life to report them all when an enraged and very famous bull rider had done it instead. Gerard Jefferson had so many bodyguards and members of the press following him around that Nate Redfern; Nate's father, Kent; and the rest of their crew, had fled.

Not fast enough, unfortunately for them. All but Redfern's father had been arrested, and only because Kent Redfern had managed to convince everyone that he was old, feeble, and innocent of his son's misdeeds. He wasn't, Hal knew damn well, but Kent's lawyers had been persuasive.

Hal had been the person, in fact, who'd alerted Jefferson, the top rider of the circuit at that time, to what was happening. Hal had offered to go with Jefferson to report the crimes, but Jefferson had said flatly that Hal would be dead if he did. Jefferson had the clout, the connections, and the protection to keep himself from harm.

So, Hal had backed off and let Jefferson be the hero. Hal had quit riding and found a remote town to retreat to, turning to ranch managing for his day job and being a rodeo clown when the circuit came through. As a clown—or bullfighter as they preferred to be called—he could help his fellow riders but be more or less anonymous to the spectators in the stands.

He'd heard that Redfern had been tried and convicted, but his sentence must not have been harsh enough.

"You out on parole?" Hal asked. "You should probably get yourself back to San Angelo, right?"

Redfern's grin didn't waver, but his eyes hardened. "I'm not on parole. My sentence was reduced, and I finished it. I'm done. Never going back."

Hal lifted his beer and drank without answering. He guessed that Redfern's prison time had been cut short because he'd turned on his friends and claimed they'd done the bulk of the dirty work. Redfern had tried to shove some blame onto Hal as well, but Jefferson and his lawyers had protected him.

"New town, new life," Redfern said. "Which you are going to help me with."

Hal nonchalantly took another sip of beer, though his heartbeat quickened in anger. "Nope. I'm not."

To his surprise, Redfern didn't press the issue. "I get why you like it here. It's quiet. You can walk down the middle of the street, and no one will run you over."

"No one sober will," Hal corrected him. "I'd watch it after this bar closes." Plus, sometimes strangers barreled through town, convinced Riverbend's roads were shortcuts to somewhere else.

Redfern tipped his mug to Hal. "I'll keep that in mind." He slurped, foam clinging to his upper lip, then his eyes brightened. "Things just got more interesting in here, I tell you."

Hal swung around to see what had caught Redfern's attention. A group of women had entered and made their way toward one of the tables, waving and returning greetings to those who called to them.

Most of the ladies were Campbell wives—Bailey and Christina, Jess and Callie. With them was Lucy. *Shit.*

For the evening Lucy had donned a red, glittery, tight-fitting tank top over a slim pair of jeans. She'd thrown a loose long-sleeved shirt over her top, as the March nights were still cold, but it couldn't hide her sexy curves. Her dark hair was a riot of short curls, and her red-lipsticked mouth curved at something Jess had just said to her.

Hal was so intent on Lucy and the heat that seared

through him that he missed Redfern deserting his stool and approaching the group.

Though Hal knew of Redfern's evilness, the man understood how to charm women. They fell for him, despite him being a sloppily dressed asshole, and many of his conquests had been dumbfounded when he'd been arrested.

"Evening." Redfern greeted the ladies. He'd removed his Astros cap and managed to look guileless. "Forgive my forwardness, but I'm new in town. Can you recommend me somewhere to eat?"

Callie and Bailey, both full of sunny goodness, started to answer. Jess, with her keener knowledge of the world, glowered at him, as did Christina. Both Jess and Christina had worked for years in bars and had come to recognize a smooth-talking dickhead when they saw one.

Lucy regarded Redfern with puzzled interest and joined Callie and Bailey in her willingness to answer. All three agreed he should go to Mrs. Ward's diner.

Redfern zeroed in on Lucy. "That's the one across the lot, isn't it?" He stepped casually closer to Lucy in an unspoken request for her to guide him.

"It sure is," Lucy answered. "It—"

She cut off with startled gasp as Hal thrust his large form between her and Redfern. "Get out," Hal stated to him.

The five ladies stared in surprise but said nothing. They were trusting Hal's judgement in the situation, which gave him a warm feeling behind his rage.

"Calm down, cowboy," Redfern said affably. "I was just asking for directions."

"No," Hal said. "You were just getting the hell out of here."

"Yeah?" Redfern's voice hardened the slightest bit, a tone

Hal knew meant he wanted a fight. "Let's ask the ladies if they want me to stay." He turned to Lucy. "Name's Nate, sugar. Want to get out of here and find some— *Uhrp*."

The question came to a gurgling halt as Hal closed his hand around Redfern's throat and lifted the man off his feet.

CHAPTER FIVE

Lucy gaped in astonishment as Hal—the affable, slow-smiling, never-says-a-harsh-word Hal Jenkins—glared up at Nate hanging from his massive grip. Nate's eyes bulged as Hal began to squeeze.

"Hal," Bailey tried to protest, but Hal ignored her.

The others were strangely silent. Lucy tore her gaze from Hal to see that Christina and Jess had closed in front of Bailey, both with folded arms and hard-ass stances. Callie had vanished.

Lucy's throat went dry. First, Hal had been oddly cold to her and Dr. Anna, and now he was strangling a stranger in the bar.

No, not a stranger, Lucy realized. Hal scowled up at the man in angry recognition. Hal knew this Nate and hated him. Hated him enough to seriously hurt him if not stopped. Nate clawed at Hal's hand, legs churning as he struggled to breathe.

"Is there a problem?" The quiet question came from Ross Campbell. Callie shadowed him, which explained where she'd disappeared to. She must have slipped out of the bar to find her husband, the sheriff, who'd lingered in the parking lot with his brothers.

Nate coughed. "Get him off me," he pleaded.

"Jenkins," Ross said, still calm. "Put him down."

Hal didn't appear to hear him. Ross, casual in jeans and black shirt, stepped to Hal, his usual geniality fading into a businesslike stare. Ross was going to arrest him if Hal didn't listen.

"Hal," Lucy said. "Let Ross handle this, okay?"

Hal jerked his intense gaze from Nate and set it on Lucy, and she faltered. Hal's usually kind brown eyes were flinty, full of a brutal rage she'd never seen in him.

"Hal?" she asked hesitantly.

Hal blinked. The grim hardness fled his face, to her relief, which softened back into that of the man she knew.

Hal looked up at Nate's mottled red cheeks and wild eyes and slowly lowered the man to the ground. He released Nate and stepped back, but Lucy noted that Hal kept himself between her and Nate.

"Thank you," Ross said to Hal, ever polite, then turned to Nate. "Hey there. I'm Ross Campbell, Sheriff of River County. And you are?"

Nate coughed and rubbed his throat. "Sheriff? Aren't you going to arrest him?"

"Depends." Ross kept his Campbell-blue eyes on Nate. "Who did you say you were?"

"Nate Redfern." He continued to rub his throat. "Old friend of Jenkins'."

Old friend, Lucy repeated in her head. Right. Old enemies, it looked like.

"Nice to meet you." Ross ignored Hal to focus on Nate. "Tell you what. Why don't you go home to wherever you're staying tonight, and then tomorrow, if you're still in town, you come to my office and have a chat with me."

Nate bristled. "What for?"

"I'd like to get to know you." Ross's answer was easy, but he was clearly giving Nate an order.

"I'll think about it." Nate sized up Ross, his eyes taking on a calculating light before he shrugged. "Sure, might be interesting."

Ross's brows rose the slightest bit. "Might be."

Hal scowled at Nate, as though he knew what the man was thinking. "Just get out of here," Hal growled.

"Keep it cool, Jenkins. I'm talking to the sheriff." Nate took a step closer to Ross, who did not look in the least daunted. "Things must be tedious in a little town like this. Can't be very lucrative, either."

Wait a minute—was Nate hinting that he would slip Ross a bribe? Lucy wondered in amazement. He didn't know much about Riverbend, did he?

What Nate also didn't know was that Ross, sheriff or not, had four older and larger brothers, and one in particular was very protective of Ross. That brother—Carter Sullivan, a former foster teen adopted by the Campbell boys' mother—materialized out of nowhere to breathe down Nate's neck.

"I'll see you tomorrow," Ross told Nate. His cheerful tone belied the steel in his voice. "I suggest you go now."

Nate peered over his shoulder at Carter then glanced at Hal. Behind Hal, Jack Hillman, more biker than cowboy, sauntered over, sensing potential trouble. He halted at Hal's back, and Nate's ingenuous expression started to fade.

"Not a very welcoming place, is it?" Nate said to Ross. "I was just having a drink, minding my own business. But okay." He held up his hands and made a show of backing away. "My review on Yelp is going to be pretty harsh." He shot a wink at Lucy, as though hoping she'd like his humor and join his side. Lucy gave him a faint shake of her head.

Nate didn't seem discouraged but nonchalantly turned away and started for the door, as if leaving had been his decision.

Two more Campbell brothers—Tyler and Grant—flanked Nate to escort him out. Carter and Jack followed, and Hal started after them, but Ross quietly stepped in front of Hal.

"I'd like to talk to you tomorrow too, Jenkins. When it's convenient. At Circle C though, not the sheriff's office. Informal, say around five. I'm cooking."

Ross's tone was genuinely friendly, but Lucy could see he meant the invitation as a command. Hal hesitated, not happy, but he gave Ross a nod.

"He's trouble," Hal told him in a low voice.

"I got that." Ross half turned to slide his arm around Callie's waist. "But we'll talk about it tomorrow. Enjoy your night."

Morphing from River County Sheriff to loving husband, he walked away with Callie.

Lucy found herself relatively alone with Hal. The Campbell wives had moved to follow their husbands and brothers-in-law, as though wanting to make sure they kept everything under control.

Hal remained in front of Lucy, the anger Lucy had sensed in him yesterday morning still in him. She thought she understood now—this Nate must have charged into town to give Hal a hard time, and Hal was pissed off about it.

She wasn't sure why his fury at Nate had made him so rude to her and Anna, but life could be complicated. There was obviously more between Hal and Nate than met the eye.

Nate was a con artist. *That* Lucy recognized. She'd met plenty of them in the stockbroking business, men and women both, who would chatter with you like you were their new best friend, all the while luring you into their trap. Nate wasn't wearing a business suit and hadn't invited her to a five-star restaurant with a view, but he gave off the same vibe.

Hal continued to say nothing. At least he wasn't shutting her out this time, but the silence was becoming awkward.

"Let's forget about him." Lucy took a step to Hal, trying to decide how to comfort him. How would she with any other of her friends? Or her brothers?

No, not her brothers. She could never, ever think of Hal as a brother.

"How about we dance?" Lucy asked.

The band had begun a fast-paced tune, and couples were already whizzing around in the two-step or quick waltz. A fast dance meant they didn't have to touch much if Hal didn't want to.

Hal stared at Lucy in astonishment, as though she'd suggested he juggle a set of chairs.

"No, I gotta go." Hal's cheeks darkened, and he cleared his throat. "You be careful tonight, all right? Don't go home alone."

Lucy tried to hide the disappointment that bit her. "No one here I want to go home with." She hoped she could tease him into some banter, not that he really was into that. But at least he might smile.

Hal's mouth firmed. "I mean, don't walk home alone. I'm serious."

"I understand." Lucy glanced to the door where Nate had just exited, followed by the Campbell brothers and Jack. "He's bad news. I don't have to be the sheriff to figure that out. Don't worry, I won't wait for him in a dark alley so I can ask what the deal is between you two."

"Don't ask him anything," Hal said sharply. "Don't talk to him. Don't even look at him."

"I won't." Lucy's irritation rose. "I'm not an idiot. I'm a Malory, and I've lived in the evil big cities. I know when a guy is on the con. Ross will send him packing, and you won't have to worry about him anymore."

If she thought she'd soothe him, Lucy was wrong. Hal's scowl, which would scare anyone but Lucy, creased his face.

"Stay out of this," he stated. "Just trust me."

With that, Hal turned and walked away. He ignored the beer he'd left on the bar, grabbed his hat from the hook where he'd hung it, and banged out the door.

Lucy stared after him, open-mouthed. She was aware that others were watching, some in gleeful interest.

Let them speculate. Lucy had never seen Hal so upset or so worried. She needed to know what was going on and what she could do about it. Even if Hal grew angry at her, even if she and Hal could never be more than friends, she refused to sit by and wring her hands while this Nate was threatening Hal.

She'd round up the town if she had to, to make sure Nate left Hal alone. Lucy might have fled Riverbend for the wider world, but she was a Riverbender at heart, from one of its prominent families, and she'd stop at nothing to keep Hal safe.

———

REDFERN WAS NOWHERE IN SIGHT WHEN HAL STORMED from the bar. Nor were the Campbells, for that matter, or Jack.

Maybe they were escorting Redfern to the edge of town to toss him out. Would be nice.

Redfern, however, was a wily S.O.B., and was probably even now figuring out ways around the Campbells, including Ross. Ross was very young to be a county sheriff, and Hal imagined Nate's wheels spinning about ways to discredit him or to make him dance to Nate's tune.

Hal drew a breath in the chill darkness of the parking lot. It was Saturday night, so the bar and its lot were full. Couples held each other in the shadows, many of them parents happy they had a babysitter so they could act like teenagers for one night.

His world had stopped when Nate had approached Lucy. Hal hadn't even thought about what he'd do—he'd just known he had to get Nate away from her. Nate had implied on the phone that he knew about Lucy, and what he had planned could not be good.

Lucy, as she'd pointed out, wasn't stupid and wouldn't fall for Redfern's bullshit. Hal knew that, and he admired her for it. But Redfern was dangerous. He'd try to use Lucy any way he could to get at Hal. If Redfern couldn't beguile her, he'd move on to threats—both to her and her family—and then to violence.

Ross expected Hal to tamely go home tonight and then toddle to visit him tomorrow at the ranch and tell him the entire story. Hal would tell him, yes, but there was no way he could stay at his place, maybe finish a beer while he watched TV, and then settle down to a dreamless sleep.

Lucy had remained in the bar, probably even now complaining about Hal's rudeness to her friends. When she was ready, she'd leave and walk home, as was her habit. She might or might not take his warning about not going alone.

Redfern was somewhere out here. Unless the Campbell brothers broke all his limbs or Ross threw him in jail, he'd be back. And he already had Lucy in his sites.

Hal pulled his jacket closer over his chest against the cooling night, hunkered against the wall of the bar, and waited.

Lucy emerged a few hours later. It was still fairly early, only about ten, but she walked out with Bailey, the two ladies laughing together. Hal kept his place in the shadows as the two headed through the parking lot and to the empty street that led to Lucy's home.

He quietly followed.

Halfway down Lucy's street the pair stopped. Bailey hugged her, then chirped open the lock of a small pickup and climbed into it, Bailey heading home.

Lucy waved as the truck drove off, then resumed her walk. She was only a few houses from her own, and she strode quickly, not lingering. Keys jingled as she clenched them in her hand, ready to unlock the door the instant she reached it.

Hal watched, becoming another shadow in the shadows, until Lucy opened her door, went inside, and switched on a light.

Lucy was inside and safe. Hal decided to wait a while longer, in the darkness under a tree near Mrs. Kaye's porch. He wanted to make sure Redfern too wasn't watching from another vantage point until Lucy put out the light and went to sleep.

The windows in the rear of Lucy's house glowed. The kitchen was in the back—Hal had helped on enough repair work in these small shotgun houses to know how they were laid out. Living room first, then bedroom, bath, and kitchen. Lucy must be getting herself a snack or maybe some coffee or a drink of water.

"I see you down there, Hal Jenkins." The voice that startled Hal belonged to Lucy's neighbor, Mrs. Kaye, but her tone was quiet, as though she knew Hal didn't want to be discovered. "Instead of lurking in the bushes, why don't you come on up to the porch?"

Hal stepped out from under the tree—a cherry tree, which would bloom in pink glory next month. He mounted the steps, and then did his best to meld into the darkness beyond the porch light.

"Sorry if I scared you," Hal said to Mrs. Kaye.

Mrs. Kaye was dressed in sweatpants and jacket, her gray hair tied in a ponytail. "You didn't. Why are you stalking Lucy? Why don't you just go knock on her door?"

"Not stalking." Hal winced, realizing that's what this could look like. "Making sure she's safe."

"Without her knowing."

Hal shrugged. "Better this way."

"Mmm-hmm." Mrs. Kaye's keen glance pierced him. "Young people can be obtuse these days, but I get it. You want to make sure she's all right. But Lucy will be annoyed if she knows and insist she doesn't need looking after. She's wrong, of course."

Hal regarded her in surprise. "You think so?"

Mrs. Kaye gave him a sage nod. "She's a young woman on her own. Vulnerable after what happened to her at her job with that awful man she was seeing. She thinks she's fine, but she's not thinking straight. Besides, it's dangerous for a woman to live alone, even in Riverbend. You can never be sure who's around."

True enough. "You live alone, Mrs. Kaye," Hal pointed out.

"I know, sweetie, but I'm tough. I know everyone in town

and will have half of them over here as soon as I yell. Plus, no one messes with me."

Also true. Mrs. Kaye was diminutive, chattered a lot, and liked to bake things for her church and the school fundraisers, but she was no pushover.

"I'm sorry if I disturbed you," Hal said.

"I don't mind a bit of company. If you want to stick around and make sure Lucy's all right, you might as well get comfortable. That chair is big enough for you and I'll fetch you a blanket. It's chilly tonight."

Mrs. Kaye pointed to a cushioned porch chair in the corner, one deep in shadow. Hal glanced at it, tempted.

"I don't want to put you to any trouble," he said. "This is my deal. I'll work it out."

Mrs. Kaye sniffed. "You'd rather shiver in the flowerbed and catch cold than sit up here with a warm blanket and a cup of coffee? I never thought you were that silly."

The woman was going to insist. And she was right—if Hal felt the need to watch over Lucy, Mrs. Kaye's front porch was the perfect spot from which to do it.

"All right," he conceded. "But if I'm in the way, you kick me out, okay?"

"How will you be in the way in a corner of the porch?" Mrs. Kaye scoffed. "Besides, you'll be watching over my house too. A bit of protection is always welcome."

Moments ago, she'd insisted she was fine by herself. Hal supposed she was being nice, making it seem like Hal was doing her a favor.

Without another word, Mrs. Kaye slipped back into the house. Hal made his way to the porch chair and sank down into it, admitting to himself that it was comfy.

Mrs. Kaye returned in a brief time with a thick knitted

blanket and an extra cushion for Hal's back. Another jaunt inside while Hal set up the chair produced a bright-colored travel mug of hot coffee.

"If you need anything, you just knock on the window," Mrs. Kaye said. "Good night, Hal."

Hal nodded, torn between embarrassment and gratitude. "Thanks, Mrs. Kaye."

"And I won't say a word to Lucy." Mrs. Kaye touched her lips, sending Hal a conspiratorial look. "This will be our secret."

Hal had to smile. "I appreciate that."

With another nod, Mrs. Kaye retreated and shut the door. Hal heard her turn on music, a cross between country and rock, her voice rising as she started to sing along.

Hal sipped the coffee, which was very good, and settled in to make sure Redfern didn't come anywhere near Lucy's house.

When Hal had lived in San Angelo and followed the rodeo circuit, he'd been friends with some very tough men. They'd been hard-assed and hadn't put up with any shit. Hal had fit right in.

Those friends would laugh themselves sick if they could see Hal now, tucked up on a porch chair with a floral-patterned blanket and matching cushions, drinking coffee from a pink mug with the words *Hey, I'm gorgeous*, on it.

They could eat shit, Hal decided. He'd put up with anything if it kept Redfern far away from Lucy.

———

LUCY STEPPED ONTO HER FRONT PORCH IN THE MORNING, ready for a lazy Sunday. A slight noise made her turn to the house on her right, where she saw Mrs. Kaye on *her* porch, folding up a blanket and tucking a pillow on top of it.

Interesting. Maybe she'd come out here early to watch the sunrise.

"Morning, Mrs. Kaye," Lucy called, and waved.

"Good morning, Lucy. How are you?"

"A little worried, actually." Lucy hadn't slept much during the night. "About Hal."

"Are you?" Mrs. Kaye fixed on her with interest. "What are you going to do about it?"

Lucy slid her phone from her pocket and gazed at its dark face. "I tried calling him, but it went to voice mail. Maybe it's too early."

"You could go see him," Mrs. Kaye said, a little too casually.

Lucy continued to stare at her phone. Hal lived on a narrow lane off FM Road 231A, halfway between town and the ranch where he worked. A pleasant drive on a weekend.

She raised her head and met Mrs. Kaye's waiting gaze. "I could," Lucy said. "I think I will."

"Right away," Mrs. Kaye said.

Lucy smothered a choked laugh at the woman's adamance. "Sure, why not? See you, Mrs. Kaye."

"Good." Mrs. Kaye beamed as Lucy tripped down the porch steps and opened the door of her small car. "Tell him I said hello."

CHAPTER SIX

Lucy wasn't entirely sure how Mrs. Kaye had talked her into driving out of Riverbend and heading for Hal's house, but here she was.

There were a few homes down this side road off FM 231A, built long ago by people wanting to escape the bustle of Riverbend. Some might laugh now that Riverbend had been considered "bustling," but before everyone had started using big box stores or ordering everything online, Riverbend on a weekend had been a jumping place. Lucy remembered Saturdays when all the outlying ranchers would come to town, clearing out the hardware store and small grocery marts, then packing the diner and bar.

Small towns were dying out in that way. On the other hand, people tired of the stress of the cities were buying up houses and properties where they could retire, or work remotely, or simply take a summer or weekend retreat. Karen Marvin was doing great business selling real estate to individual owners, and at the same time, working hard to keep mass developers out.

The trouble with the road Hal lived on was that it didn't go much of anywhere. It ended at the river, but not in an accessible place for swimming or hiking, or even for gazing at the view. It simply ended. Therefore, Lucy couldn't pretend she was on her way to somewhere else and had stopped to see him in passing.

She gripped the steering wheel as she took the curves under the huge oak trees, cool wind pouring through her open windows. Oh, well, she'd come this far. She'd have to think of some excuse.

Hal's truck was parked in his carport attached to the house, meaning he was home. Lucy's nervousness rose. If he wasn't at the ranch or out running around helping everyone in the county, why hadn't he answered his phone? It was already ten, and Hal, she knew, was an early riser.

Lucy made herself not overthink what she was doing. She parked her car, closed the windows in case the gathering clouds in the east decided to dump rain, turned off the ignition, and climbed out.

She realized halfway up the path to the front door that she should have stopped at Grace's bakery and grabbed some pastries. Of course, Grace didn't open until noon on Sunday, and she would also want to know exactly why Lucy wanted the pastries and who they were for.

Lucy also ought to have waited and devised a plan with several reasonable explanations instead of rushing out here without thought. She had no idea what she was going to say to Hal, no clue what excuse she'd have for arriving without warning.

Oh well, if Hal was watching Lucy approach the door, she couldn't very well run away now. He'd think she was nuts. He probably thought that already, but why reinforce the idea?

When Lucy had worked for Clyde's father's company, she'd made some of her best deals simply going with her gut. She'd been good, knowing exactly when to talk a client into an investment and when to warn them away. She *had* been good, and Clyde had been an idiot to fire her.

The thought of Clyde galvanized Lucy into action. "Eff it," she told herself as she halted on the doorstep. "I'm doing this. I'm just talking to a friend, seeing if he's all right."

She drew a breath and knocked on the solid door set between the small brick home's two front windows.

Her knock echoed into the house, which responded with silence. Lucy's pulse sped as she lingered on the porch. She'd called, and Hal hadn't answered. He must know who it was out here knocking, and he wasn't rushing to open the door.

Hal was sending her big "stay away" signals...was she too dense to get that?

Or was something wrong? Hal was, above all, excruciatingly polite. Even if Lucy were the last person on the planet he wanted to see, he'd respond, even if only to tell her he was okay and that she could leave him alone.

Alarm growing, Lucy knocked on the door again, harder this time. If she continued to get no response, she was calling Ross.

"Just a second," came a rumble from the depths of the house. "I can only move so fast."

Lucy's hand was still upraised when the door was wrenched open by an exasperated Hal.

He wore nothing but a pair of jeans, which left his feet, broad chest, and shoulders bare. His torso, face, and hair were dripping wet as he stared down at Lucy, who gaped up at him, her heart pounding. Blood flowed hot through her body as she took in his muscular form, wiry hair on his chest damp from a shower, droplets of water glistening on his skin.

"*Shit,*" Hal said.

———

IT WAS LIKE HE'D STEPPED INTO THE MIDDLE OF A RODEO ring, stark naked, with a brilliant spotlight illuminating him for all to see.

Lucy, beautiful in the dappled shade, her green eyes wide, gaped at him from his front step.

Dimly, in the back of his mind, Hal wondered what the hell she was doing here. In the front of his mind was the fact that she was breathtaking in slim pants and a close-fitting T-shirt. Also, that water dripped from his legs under his jeans to pool on his slate floor.

He'd just stepped out of the shower when he heard the knock. He hadn't been sure if it was Ross wanting to talk to him early about Nate, Nate himself, or a rancher who needed help. No matter what, he'd grabbed his jeans and shoved them on, striding for the door.

He was bare-assed under them, which wouldn't have mattered if anyone else had been on his doorstep.

"Shit," he said again.

Lucy closed her mouth, her eyes taking on an irritated light. "Good morning to you too."

"Uh ..." Hal groped for an intelligent response, but his brain and his tongue weren't communicating with each other. "I—uh—was in the shower."

"So I see." Lucy's gaze moved from his wet hair down his body to his damp bare toes.

Hal's flesh scalded in the wake of her onceover. It was as

though she'd run her tongue from his neck to his feet … and *damn,* he shouldn't think of things like that. Not when only one layer of fabric separated him from her.

"Sorry." He spied a T-shirt hanging from the back of a nearby chair and made a grab for it. He missed.

"I have two brothers," Lucy informed him from the threshold. "They weren't always careful about shutting doors when we were growing up. Trust me, I've seen it all. More than I ever wanted to."

"This is probably a little more than you wanted today." Hal reached for the shirt again, this time snagging it, and held it bunched in front of his chest.

"It's not bad." Lucy tilted her head to study him, and Hal swore his entire body blushed.

"What are you doing here?" In a rush, Hal remembered what the sight of her had wiped from his brain—that being around him was dangerous. "You shouldn't have come."

Lucy's annoyance returned. "Like I said, good morning to you too. I came to see if you were all right. That complete asshole from the bar last night might have tracked you down. You didn't answer your phone, and I got worried."

The fact that she worried about him made something blossom in Hal's heart. "He hasn't come near me. I overslept."

He'd driven carefully home after watching over Lucy's house all night, locked his doors, fallen into bed, and slept hard. When intense sunlight had awakened him, he'd dragged himself into the shower.

"That's not like you," Lucy said. "From what I hear, you're up at the crack of dawn, even on holidays."

"Habit of the job." Animals woke with the sun, sometimes before it, and didn't understand about waiting for meals or care.

"You don't have to explain." Lucy leaned against the doorframe. "Are you going to let me stand here in the doorway? Either tell me to go away or invite me in."

"I don't want you to go away." The truth sprang from Hal's lips before he could stop it. "But it's not safe around me. Not with Redfern in the area."

"I'm not afraid of him." Lucy rested her arm above her head, which stretched the T-shirt in sexy ways. "Ross and his brothers will take care of him. Not to mention *my* brothers. He won't bother you for long."

She was both right and wrong. The Campbells and Malorys would clan together to keep Lucy safe, but Redfern was a canny guy. He wouldn't overtly attack, not yet. He'd wait until he thought he had the advantage, and then he'd go for it. He'd come for Hal sooner or later, and Redfern had already sized up Lucy as way to get to Hal.

Redfern had been rattled by last night's encounter with the Campbell family, enough to leave the bar without a fight, but he'd even now be figuring out how to go around them to get to Hal.

"Should I leave?" Lucy asked when Hal didn't answer. The question was casual, but Hal read tension in her eyes.

The idea that Hal could hurt her was new. He pushed aside the need to review this interesting fact and cleared his throat.

"No, please come on in," he said. "I'll go get decent."

Lucy's smile broke through her annoyance, the one that made Hal forget his own name. "I'd say you were already decent. Want me to make you breakfast? Or we could go into town to the diner."

Hal's limbs turned to jelly. The choice was to have her all to himself in his own kitchen, or to go with her to the diner where he'd have to share her with everyone else in town.

"Sure, we could stay here," he managed to answer. "You don't have to cook for me, though. I got it."

"I drove all the way out here to be nice to you." Lucy slid past him into the house, the warmth of her passing not helping his shakiness. "Not to be catered to. I can't whip up a meal like one of Grace's—she was born with all the cooking genes—but she's taught me some things. What's in your fridge?"

Lucy had never been to Hal's home before, but she walked straight to the kitchen without guidance. Not that the house's layout was a big mystery. The door opened straight into the living room, and the kitchen lay behind it. A short hall off the living room led to two compact bedrooms with a bathroom between them.

Lucy gazed around the small kitchen which was mostly a U-shaped counter flanked by a stove on one side and a refrigerator on the other. A few cabinets lined the walls. "This is cute."

"I don't need much. I'm not here a lot."

"I know. You practically live at Kennedy's ranch." She turned to him, her dark hair glimmering in the light from the back window. "I've always wondered why you don't actually live there. Mr. Kennedy is a nice guy—he'd find you a decent trailer onsite, I'd bet."

Hal shrugged. Kennedy had offered him a comfortable mobile home that the last manager had used, but Hal had refused.

"I like my own space, I guess."

"I hear you." Lucy gave him a fervent nod. "That's why I moved into Anna's place instead of bunking at the Malory family home. I love our ranch, but at the same time ..." She opened her hands in a helpless gesture. "Nice to be able to close the door and think about stuff, am I right?"

Her every movement was graceful. Hal hated that he hadn't been able to take her up on her offer of a dance last night. Having Lucy in his arms, or even simply holding her hands, would have made a lot of his past hurting go away.

"Yeah. Exactly." Hal folded his arms, the T-shirt still bunched in his hand. He watched her skim through the kitchen, opening cupboards, checking the fridge, familiarizing herself with everything.

Hal had a sudden vision of Lucy being here for always. He'd wake in the morning to find her in the kitchen, bathing him in her nearness while she scrounged breakfast for the two of them. Or leaning on the counter while she watched *him* cook. Then they'd sit across from each other at the small table while they read the morning news or chatted over coffee before heading out to their respective jobs. Then at night, they'd come home, share another meal, and head to bed ...

He wanted all this with a sudden intensity, more than he'd ever wanted anything in his life.

Lucy turned, raised her brows when she saw Hal unmoving in the doorway, and made a shooing gesture.

"Go on," she commanded. "Finish drying off. I'll figure something out."

Hal spent a few more seconds bathing his senses in her before he pivoted on his heel to head to his bedroom. He slipped on a puddle he'd created, started to fall, and barely caught himself on the kitchen doorframe.

A gentle but steady hand on his shoulder almost made his leg slide out from under him completely.

Hal turned cautiously, his back against the doorframe, but Lucy didn't step away. Instead, she was in front of him, her hands resting on his shoulders, her body an enticing inch from his.

"Careful," she said softly.

Hal abruptly found it hard to breathe.

The kiss Hal had shared with Lucy at the B&B's opening celebration flashed through his thoughts. He remembered with searing clarity how she'd slid her arms around his neck and how he'd bent to touch her lips in a brief but scorching kiss.

From the darkening of her eyes, Lucy remembered it too.

Her touch soothed him, and before Hal realized it, the inch between them was gone. Lucy's T-shirt brushed his bare skin, the shirt Hal had grabbed dangling uselessly from his hand.

Lucy rose to him, her gaze holding an inquiry. She wasn't going to take what Hal wasn't willing to give, but she'd ask for it. Lucy wasn't the shy Malory sister.

To Hal, she was the most beautiful one. Smothering a groan, Hal tipped her face toward his, scooped her against his body, and took her mouth in a hard kiss.

CHAPTER SEVEN

Lucy suppressed her start of delight. She hadn't been able to stop herself melding into Hal as he'd steadied himself in the doorway, but she'd expected him to push her off and walk away.

His strong hands on her waist, his mouth embracing hers, told her Hal didn't want to walk away.

Lucy wound her arms around his neck and parted her lips, stroking his strong shoulders to pull him closer. Their first kiss last year had been intense but fleeting, lighting flames inside that hadn't yet gone out.

This kiss doubled the intensity of the first. Heat rose within her, blotting out everything but Hal's body against hers, the beads of water on his skin dampening her shirt.

Hal cupped her cheek and slid his hand under her hair. Lucy leaned into him, letting him hold her steadily while she kissed and kissed him. His wet hair danced under her fingers, showering more droplets over them.

Lucy shivered happily at the feeling, but Hal didn't break

the kiss. He pulled her tighter, as though he didn't notice they were getting soaked.

More than Lucy's shirt was growing wet. Fire built between her legs, a desire she hadn't felt in a very long time.

Lucy broke the kiss to lick the hollow of Hal's throat.

He made a soft noise, his grip on her tightening as he tilted his head back so she could brush dampness from his skin. She followed up with more kisses across his collarbone.

Still holding her, Hal edged into the living room, while Lucy kissed his neck, shoulders, throat. It wasn't far until Lucy's feet met the area rug, and a moment after that, they more or less fell into an armchair.

Lucy ended up on Hal's lap, where he gathered her into his arms. She turned to face him, her knees going around his thighs.

Their kisses became fierce. They were going to go for it, Lucy realized. Maybe not here on this chair, but right now, this morning, in Hal's house. The excitement of that knowledge fanned the flames higher, anticipation a heady aphrodisiac.

No matter what happened, Lucy planned to enjoy what she could. She broke their next frantic kiss, both to catch her breath and to run her fingers down Hal's bare chest.

His wiry hair caught her fingertips, and his flat nipples firmed to her touch. Lucy leaned down and licked one.

Hal let out a groan, cupping Lucy's head as she went from licking to suckling. Hal tasted warm and a little salty, the water from the shower a pleasing contrast.

"Damn," he whispered.

Lucy felt her shirt inching up, Hal's work-roughened hands on her bare skin.

But why not? Hal was bare-chested—why shouldn't she be? Lucy quickly skimmed her shirt off over her head. She

wore a silky pink bra that she unfastened for him—his big
fingers might not manage the catches quickly enough.

The admiring light in Hal's eyes was very flattering as the
bra fell away, searing her to the bone. Lucy pressed against
him, liking the feel of his hard chest under her breasts.

More kisses stoked the fire. Hal's hands on her back
showed her his strength, but also the gentleness he could tame
himself to.

Lucy slid her hand between them and opened the button
of his jeans.

Hal caught her wrist. "Sure you want to do that?"

"Hmm." Lucy touched her other finger to the side of her
mouth. "Let me think."

"It's just, I don't have anything on under there."

Lucy had suspected as much, but his confirmation made
her heart jump. "All the better," she said, trying to keep her
voice steady.

Hal's grip was firm, but Lucy stroked his fingers until he
loosened them from her wrist. Giving him a smile, she finished
prying the button open and then slid his zipper carefully
downward.

Yes, he certainly was bare under there. Lucy's heartbeat
was off the charts as she wriggled her hand inside the warm
denim and touched his bare cock.

Hal jumped. His hand returned to her wrist, his eyes
widening. Lucy stilled, her gaze locked with Hal's.

She read desire in his eyes and the same anticipation she
felt, but also apprehension. Not because of what she was
doing, necessarily, but about where this thing between them
was going. If it was a thing, and if it was going anywhere.

Lucy feared to say anything—one wrong word, and Hal
might set her on her feet, shove her clothes at her, and steer her

toward the door. She'd indicated what she wanted—now to see what he would do.

Slowly, Hal peeled his fingers from Lucy's wrist. She smothered a sigh of relief before she let her fingers softly dance on his skin.

"Hell," he said.

"It's hot enough to be," Lucy murmured.

"I don't know. I think it's a nice day ... myself." The last word was forced out. Hal squeezed his eyes shut as Lucy stroked her way down.

Hal was a large man, which meant everything was big. Lucy delighted in the length of him, found the warm firmness at the base of his cock, which meant he was ready and willing.

Lucy touched kisses to his mouth while she ran her fingers up the shaft, dancing fingertips over the head.

"Dangerous," Hal said, his eyes still tightly closed.

Lucy kissed the corner of his eyelid. "I'll say."

She continued playing, brushing kisses to his cheek. Hal opened his eyes, and the tender look he gave her wrenched her inside out.

After a moment, she felt the button of *her* pants opening, and Hal's big hand on her zipper.

"Stop me if you want to," he said in a low voice.

"Stop you?" Lucy gazed at him in amazement. "No way."

Hal fixed her with his quiet gaze. "Just giving you options."

"I'll take *this* option." Lucy closed her fingers around his hand and guided it inside her waistband.

She sucked in a breath when Hal's strong touch slid into her silky panties and between her legs and exhaled a groan.

She was ready. More than ready.

Lucy continued stroking Hal, completely coming undone as he found her heat and caressed it. His fingers were magical, propelling wildfire through her. She couldn't help rocking on his hand, any idea of decorousness fleeing.

Hal lifted his hips, responding to her touch. He moved his fingers faster on her, as though wanting her to burst into flame.

They held and stroked, kissed and groaned, until Lucy dropped her head back and let out a shriek. She was coming, brought to life by his touch. Sensations poured through her, heat and madness, joy and excitement.

She heard her voice echoing in the small house, and in the back of her mind, decided it was a good thing his nearest neighbor was a few miles away.

Hal held her in strong arms. They rocked together as she rode it out, and then she was flat against him, kissing him hard. His hot response trickled over her hand where she still gripped him.

The kisses went on, the feverish strength easing as both Hal and Lucy slowly subsided.

They ended up with Lucy lying against him, their arms around each other. Lucy's face ached from the broad grin on it.

She feared breaking the moment, even to suggest they take it into the bedroom. Or back to the shower, so Hal could clean up. That could grow interesting ...

Hal's phone buzzed on the table beside him, reality trickling back into their private sanctuary.

"Crap," Hal stated.

Lucy blinked hazily, but she didn't let go of Hal. She remained firmly in his lap, her arms around him, her lips raw from their kisses. The rest of the house was quiet, the breeze outside stirring leaves in the tall trees.

"I know you have to get that," Lucy said in resignation.

Hal was responsible for an entire ranch of cattle, and any

problems on a Sunday required him to drive out there and fix them. The steers wouldn't care that Hal wanted a day off.

"Yeah, I do." Hal reluctantly picked up the phone. Lucy saw the screen, which told her the caller was Ross Campbell.

Her haziness ebbed quickly. Ross had asked Hal to come over and talk to him about Nate, but that was later this afternoon. Did he want to see Hal right now? And why? What had changed?

Hal slowly thumbed the phone on and answered, "Hey."

"Hal." Ross's voice, which came clearly to Lucy, held his stern professional tones. This wasn't a friend calling for a chat. "Where are you?"

"Home," Hal answered. "I'm off Sundays. Mostly."

"How long have you been there?" Ross demanded. "Since you left the bar last night?"

Hal glanced at Lucy, and she saw his reluctance to answer Ross in her hearing. Strange.

"Why?" Hal countered.

"Nate Redfern was beaten up sometime last night or early this morning," Ross stated. "Beaten up bad. He's in the hospital. How about you come see me at my office, and we have that talk about him now?"

CHAPTER EIGHT

Lucy stared at Hal in shock as he hung up the phone. It was hard to pry herself from the wonderful place she'd been, drowning in pleasure and desire she hadn't felt in far too long.

The world and all its hurts, problems, and confusions had ceased to exist while she'd basked in Hal's promising kisses and his astonishingly gentle touch.

"He thinks you did it," Lucy said indignantly. Sheriff Campbell more or less accusing Hal of assaulting an icky guy from his past was not the reality she'd wanted to return to.

She slid from Hal's lap as he moved to stand up and looked around for her shirt. It had fallen to the floor, and Lucy winced as she bent to retrieve it. She'd been too far gone in pleasure to feel her knees cramping up.

"Maybe," Hal said in his stoic way. "But I didn't."

He picked up the T-shirt he'd been clutching when all this started and headed for the hall to the bedrooms.

"Of course, you didn't." Lucy refastened her bra and slid the shirt on over her head, calling after him as she adjusted things. "Carter Sullivan looked mad enough to kill last night. He and all the Campbells escorted Nate out of the bar. Jack Hillman was there too, and he's happy to help Carter with anything Carter wants to do. Why isn't Ross calling *them*?"

Hal didn't answer right away. Lucy heard him moving around in the bedroom at the very back of the house, so she stepped into the bathroom to wash up. She smoothed her hair in the mirror, rubbing off lipstick that had been smeared by Hal.

Hal didn't have much in his bathroom—a razor and toothbrush at the sink, hairbrush, and toothpaste tube on the counter.

Only one toothbrush. No sign of any feminine razors, hair products, makeup, or emergency tampons. This bathroom was meant for one guy and no one else.

Why did Lucy take such satisfaction that Hal obviously never expected female company?

Because she wanted him all to herself, of course. Selfish, but true.

"I don't know," Hal said behind her.

Lucy jumped, feeling guilty, though she hadn't been rifling the drawers or medicine cabinet or anything. She'd just glanced here and there.

"What?" she stammered.

"I don't know why Ross isn't calling his brothers or Jack." Hal, hands full of a change of clothes, answered the question Lucy had asked forever ago. "I guess I'll find out."

He politely moved aside to let her leave the bathroom, then he glided in and closed the door. Lucy heard the shower go back on, so Hal could clean up from their fervent play.

Lucy waited for him in the living room, observing his simply furnished house that didn't hold many photos or knickknacks. A functional sofa and the chair they'd had such fun on, a square wooden coffee table, an end table with a few magazines about farming and ranching. No lamps, just an overhead light. The only picture on the wall was a print of a painting of The Hill Country—Lucy had seen many like it in the small antique and home furnishing stores around the county. No photos of family or friends, not even one of Hal himself.

It was as if he'd purged himself of his entire past when he'd moved to Riverbend.

Not long later Hal emerged from the bathroom. He'd dressed in another pair of jeans, probably with underwear beneath them this time. He'd pulled on a button-down shirt and donned boots, like he was going to work.

He halted when he saw Lucy sitting in the living room, his surprised expression telling Lucy he hadn't expected her to still be there.

"I'm coming with you," Lucy declared.

"You don't need to." Hal sounded neither elated nor dismayed that she wanted to go. "Ross didn't know you were here when he called."

"Doesn't matter." Lucy rose and headed to the front door, where her purse waited on the table next to it. "I'm not letting Ross arrest you for something you didn't do."

"Don't worry. Ross won't arrest me without evidence."

Hal was confident, but Lucy wasn't so certain. Ross was fair and smart, but Hal had attacked Nate in the bar, and only Ross's intervention had made Hal back off. Ross would naturally think of Hal as suspect number one.

"We can't be sure of that," Lucy said. "Come on. I'll drive you."

"No need. I can take my truck."

Hal's patient responses were starting to make her crazy.

"You haven't had any breakfast," Lucy pointed out. "You'll explain to Ross and then we can go get breakfast. Or lunch." It was already almost noon.

Hal rubbed his hand through his short hair. "If I drive myself, you're going to follow me, aren't you?"

"Yep."

He blew out a breath. "Come on, then."

Lucy wasn't certain whether or not to feel triumphant. She'd won the argument—hadn't she?

She led the way out, her body still aching for him. She and Hal definitely had unfinished business.

The news that Nate was lying in a hospital bed, severely hurt, unsettled her. Lucy instinctively hadn't liked Nate—and he hadn't proved her instincts wrong—but the violence of the situation was distressing.

Hal couldn't have had anything to do with that, Lucy was certain. He didn't take shit from anyone, but he didn't need to beat someone down to gain their respect. His kindheartedness was well known. He'd half-choked Nate, yes, but even then, Lucy believed Hal would have stopped short of seriously hurting the man.

She hurried to the car, waiting until Hal had stuffed himself into the small passenger seat before she pulled from Hal's house.

The lane was empty when she turned onto it and remained so all the way to the 231A. It was a fine Sunday afternoon, and Riverbend's residents would be wherever they were spending it—hiking or fishing along the river, at home, or with friends for Sunday brunch, or hanging out at the diner, waiting for the bar to open later.

"Will you tell me about Nate?" Lucy asked as she drove past green fields and hills dotted with trees.

Hal moved his shoulders in a shrug. "I really don't want to."

"I know it's none of my business. You told me to stay out of it. Pretty sharply."

Hal folded his arms, the bulk of one touching Lucy's shoulder. "I'm sorry about that. I didn't mean to snap at you. Redfern's good at riling me up."

"Apparently." Ross would have discerned that as well. "We're friends, aren't we? Maybe more than friends?" Lucy sent him a hopeful glance. "If Nate is that dangerous, and someone even *more* dangerous let him have it, shouldn't I know about him? And what his deal is?"

Hal didn't speak for a long while. Riverbend wasn't far, but far enough for him to sit in silence for several minutes.

When he spoke, his voice was quieter than Lucy had ever heard it. "If I tell you, you won't want to be friends with me anymore."

Lucy suppressed a qualm of unease. "We'll have to risk that. Friends have to be honest with each other."

Hal moved uncomfortably. Lucy thought he'd shut her out again, but then he drew a resigned breath.

"He doped bulls," Hal said. "And horses. On the rodeo circuit. Led a pack of cowboys, including his own dad, who cheated for themselves and other riders for a powerful lot of money."

"Oh." Lucy felt sick.

In Anna's practice Lucy saw the toll that filling a horse or bull full of adrenaline or steroids or worse took on the animal. People would dope horses for increased speed on a track or bulls to make them wilder in the arena—riders got more points for the more difficult bulls. They thought nothing of tearing up an animal's internal organs to make a profit. If the horse or bull died, there was more where they came from.

It was illegal, unethical, and just plain mean. But with huge purses at stake or millions in sponsorships from corporations, a lot of people brushed the rules and laws aside.

"I tried to stop them," Hal said. "But I realized I was a lone voice in the crowd. They wanted to bribe me, first by telling me they'd make me a champion, and then with out-and-out cash. When I told them what I thought about that, they cornered me and pummeled the hell out of me, Redfern cheering his friends on with every punch. I laid low for a while, but I wasn't going to let them get away with it."

Lucy listened with growing disquiet. "Is that why you quit riding?"

"One of the reasons. Finally, I met a guy who proved to me he was well and truly against all the shit that was going on, and I told him about Redfern and his gang. He took it not only to law enforcement but also to the press. A lot of men on the board who regulated the circuit as well as local authorities had been paid off, but he knew how to get around that."

"Who was this paragon?" Lucy asked. "Why didn't *he* get bribed or beat up?"

"Gerard Jefferson."

"Ah."

Hal didn't have to explain to her who he was. Lucy's brothers were bull riders, and very good ones, but Jefferson had a special place among the riders. He was talented and he didn't cheat, which in some areas made him a remarkable person. He was also a great guy—she'd met him briefly once—but not in a weird, overly personable kind of way like Nate. He hadn't been much different in personality than Kyle or Ray.

"Well, good for Jerry Jefferson," Lucy said. "I wish he could have helped you sooner."

"He was doing a worldwide exhibition tour for a while and didn't know." Hal shrugged. "Once I told him, he got Nate and his friends shut down, arrested, and tried. Most of them spent time inside, including Nate. I don't know why they let him out of prison."

"Because he's a con artist," Lucy stated. She slowed to enter the town limits of Riverbend. "Con artists weasel their way out of anything they don't want to do, including serving time for their crimes."

Hal didn't answer. Lucy glanced at him and found him gazing at her, a half-smile on his lips. His expression shot her back to how his face had softened as he'd given into pleasure under her hands.

"What?" she asked, suppressing a frisson of delight.

"I'm glad you didn't fall for his bullshit," Hal said. "I should have known you wouldn't."

"I told you, I've been around the block. I learned my lessons the hard way—I dated a guy for years who was essentially a swindler. You know what they say: *Fool me once ...*"

His smile vanished. "Can I pop that dickhead in the mouth?"

"That would be fun. But you're already in trouble with Ross, so no."

"I did not beat up Nate," Hal repeated. "I didn't see him at all after he left the bar."

"Tell Ross that." Lucy stopped the car in front of the county courthouse where the sheriff and deputies had their offices. "I'll meet you at the diner."

Hal was staring at her in silence again. Before Lucy could

ask *What?* once more, Hal said, "I thought you'd insist on coming in with me."

Lucy's brows rose. "Sheriff Campbell isn't going to listen to *me*. Explain to him exactly what you told me about Nate, and he'll understand."

"Mmph," was Hal's only answer. He opened the car door. "If I don't come out, you'll know he locked me up."

"I'll have Grace bake a file into a cake," Lucy said, deadpan. "Though I think all the locks are electronic now. I never understood how a metal file could be baked into a cake, anyway—it would have to be a big cake, and the file would fall to the bottom."

Hal actually chuckled as he climbed out of the car. "That is true. Thanks for the lift, Lucy. See you later."

He closed the door, gave her a brief wave, and strolled along the path toward the sheriff's side of the courthouse, as though he was merely planning to meet some of his friends for morning coffee.

Lucy's optimism faded as she continued the short drive to the diner and parked in its crowded parking lot. Ross might understand that Nate was a dirtbag, but he also might not be convinced of Hal's innocence.

Hal had overslept this morning, which Lucy had reflected was unlike him. But did that mean he'd stayed out all night tracking down Nate and pounding him into the ground?

Even if Hal had done the beating, knowing Hal, he'd have driven the man to the hospital and stayed to make sure he was okay. He'd also have admitted he'd been the culprit when Ross tasked him with it.

Lucy believed Hal when he said he had nothing to do with it, plus she'd seen no evidence of bruising or abrasions on his hands, which she'd had a chance to observe up close this morning. She'd seen a lot of him up close …

Lucy shook herself from that delightful memory. There was still the troubling puzzle about where Hal had been last night and what had made him sleep so long into the morning.

———

"Morning, Hal," Mildred the dispatcher sang out as Hal entered the sheriff's department. "Though it's just about afternoon now."

Mildred, who fielded most of the distress calls in the county, pretty much knew everyone and all their business, though she was professional enough to keep it to herself.

"Morning." Hal removed his hat and stood awkwardly on the visitor's side of the counter.

The sheriff's office ran twenty-four seven, as emergencies didn't respect the clock. At mid-morning on a Sunday, however, only Mildred, whose shift rotated through the week, and one deputy—Joe Harrison—were on duty.

"How are you, Jenkins?" Harrison called across the divide from his desk.

"Not bad. You?"

"Can't complain." Harrison shrugged and gestured to the pile of folders crowding the desk's surface. "Everyone talks about the paperless office, but I think we're not seeing that in our lifetime."

"I hear you." Part of Hal's job was to keep meticulous records about the livestock at the ranch. Spreadsheets eluded him, so much of his notes were on ledgers in pencil.

Mildred turned to shout down the open hallway behind her. "Ross. Hal Jenkins is here."

"We don't need an intercom," Harrison said with a grin. "We have Mildred."

"No one's here," Mildred returned. "No reason to use the phone when Ross can hear me just fine."

Ross's voice rolled down the hall. "Send him back."

Mildred signaled Hal to open the door in the counter. Harrison sent him a friendly wave as Hal slid through and started around the desks to the hallway.

Neither Mildred nor Harrison behaved as though they believed Ross was about to arrest Hal for being a crazed assailant. Harrison did give Hal a thoughtful glance and Mildred regarded him in curiosity, but neither were alarmed.

Ross likewise waited casually for Hal, remaining seated while he scrutinized something on his computer screen. He wore civilian clothes—jeans and a shirt similar to Hal's— meaning he'd popped in on his day off.

"I was hoping to join the cookout at your mom's place," Hal said when Ross gestured him to a chair.

"You're still welcome, but things got serious, and I didn't want to wait." Ross rose and closed the door, then returned to his desk and leaned his butt against it, crossing his legs at the ankle. "I wanted to talk to you where my entire family and whatever friends they bring along can't hear."

"You want me to tell you about Redfern," Hal said. "And why I attacked him in the bar last night."

"That's a good start." Ross, the youngest Campbell, had learned to command respect at an early age by being friendly with a hint of steel behind the camaraderie. Ross was no pushover, which those who didn't know him learned in a hurry.

"I grabbed Redfern because he was going to try his bullshit

on Lucy," Hal said. "He more or less told me he'd use her to get to me. I didn't want him anywhere near her."

"I understand." Ross nodded calmly. "Ray or Kyle Malory might have done the same thing if they'd been there."

Hal's anger at Redfern hadn't been that of a brother, but he let Ross's comment stand. "You're right that I was seriously pissed off at him. So were your brothers. Sure they didn't have anything to do with this?"

"My brothers put Redfern into his truck in the parking lot and waved him off. Jack was with them, and he says the same. After that, they went back inside the bar to dance with their wives—in Carter's case, he went home to Grace. Jack claims he headed to Karen's. I already asked him."

Hal had seen Grant and Tyler drift back into the bar as he'd waited for Lucy to come out, that was true. He hadn't seen Jack or Carter at all.

"I'll be following up with Karen," Ross said. "She'll tell me truthfully whether Jack was with her or not. The only person whose whereabouts I'm not certain of is you."

Hal folded his arms. "I wasn't out beating up Redfern, I promise you. No matter what I think of him."

"You two have a past."

"Yep. We do."

"I looked up Redfern last night, and read about the doping and his conviction. Your name cropped up in his file." Ross sent Hal a watchful look. "But I want to hear your version of events. How were you involved?"

Hal let out a breath and then launched into the tale he'd told Lucy on the way into town. He'd not spoken of his days on the circuit since he'd moved to Riverbend. People had been curious about where he was from and what he did, and had plied him with questions, but eventually they'd accepted his truncated answers and left him alone.

Ross regarded Hal in silence after he finished his story. Hal knew he'd given Ross a strong motive for assaulting Redfern, but that couldn't be helped. He wanted Ross to know the truth before he heard garbled stories from those who knew only a fraction of what had happened.

"He's badly injured," Ross said after a time. "Broken ribs, broken jaw, face bruised all to hell. He's lucky he survived."

"Redfern is cruel," Hal said. "But no one deserves that. Who does *he* say beat him up?"

"He hasn't. Medical center told me he's regained consciousness, but barely. They're keeping him pretty heavily sedated, and his jaw is wired. He can't communicate as of yet."

"I have to wonder as much as you who did this," Hal said. "To my knowledge, I'm the only one in town who knows Redfern. Maybe someone from his old gang followed him here. They got heavier sentences than he did because he pointed the finger at all of them. Tried to implicate me too, but I could prove I had nothing to do with the doping."

"I thought of that—that maybe one of the guys he gave evidence against took revenge, but most of them are still in prison." Ross bent slightly toward Hal. "It would help me a lot if you told me where you were last night."

Hal fought the urge to squirm uncomfortably in the chair. Ross was about three quarters Hal's size—Hal could lift him up and throw him if he wanted to—but Ross had the upper hand in this room, and both of them knew it. The way Ross pinned him with his baby blues had Hal wishing he'd done something normal last night like gone home to bed or played pool with a dozen very reliable witnesses.

"I really can't," Hal said. "Not because I went after

Redfern, but because it involves people I don't want to drag into this."

Exasperation entered Ross's expression. "I'm trying to make sure you don't go down for it. Anything you say to me is confidential."

"Confidential," Hal repeated slowly. "Do you mean your notes will go into sealed records in a vault, or do you mean anyone in the sheriff's department will have access?"

Ross sighed. "Only those working the case will know."

"Not confidential enough, then."

"Any of the deputies can be trusted," Ross said impatiently. "Mildred included."

"Yeah? What about McGregor?"

McGregor had been a favorite of the former sheriff, whom Ross had discredited. McGregor had not been involved in his corruption and had stayed on, because Ross needed the manpower. McGregor, however, constantly let Ross know how much he resented the sheriff's removal.

"I won't assign him the case," Ross said, voice hardening.

"I can't risk that." Not only did Hal want to save Lucy the embarrassment of the town knowing he'd been watching over her that night, but Mrs. Kaye would be pulled in for questioning as well. Not fair, when neither woman had anything to do with the assault on Redfern. "You'll have to take my word for it."

"I trust you, Hal, but it's my job to be thorough. If you don't tell me, I'll have to investigate, which means questioning everyone who came into contact with you last night."

Hal peeled himself from the chair. "Then you will. You'll find out the same thing—I went nowhere near Redfern after the Campbells and Jack escorted him out, never saw him again, never touched him. This morning when you called was the first I'd heard of him getting hurt."

Ross rose to his full height. "Don't leave the county, all right?"

"Why would I? I have work tomorrow." Hal softened his tone to show he didn't blame Ross for doing his job. "Okay if I go now?"

Ross raised his brows. "Sure. If you change your mind, you know where to find me."

Hal didn't answer. He left the office with a nod of farewell to Ross and made his way back down the hall.

Mildred and Harrison were suddenly and busily concentrating on work when Hal emerged into their bullpen. He doubted they'd heard anything coming from Ross's closed office, but the innocence in their expressions told Hal they'd been listening hard.

"See you around, Jenkins," Harrison said.

"Yep," Hal answered. "Nice to talk to you, Mildred."

"Likewise," Mildred answered. Her sharp stare told Hal she had her eye on him as much as Ross did. "Take care of yourself."

"Will do."

Hal escaped the department, clapping on his hat as he walked out into the spring sunshine. He blew out a breath in relief, happy Ross hadn't marched him deeper into the building and locked him into a cell.

He paused in the town square, enjoying the breeze on his face, the scent of spring flowers blooming along the sidewalks, and watching the kids chase each other across the grass.

His gaze strayed to the diner, where Lucy's small car was parked at the edge of its lot. His thoughts flashed to Lucy's warm body on his lap, her hands bringing him easily to hardness and then to release. One of the best moments of his life, right there in his living room. Her bare body against his, her lips on his mouth, her warmth, her scent ...

A little boy yelled in delight as he ran past Hal with his friends, snapping Hal back to the present. He realized he was standing rock-still on the pavement while he daydreamed about the beauty of Lucy ... who was waiting for him even now.

He drew a breath, squared his shoulders, and started for the diner.

CHAPTER NINE

Lucy relaxed in relief when Hal made his way into the restaurant. She hadn't been certain he'd come—he could have easily found someone to give him a ride home once Ross had finished interrogating him. She'd also been worried Ross wouldn't let him go at all.

Hal paused to remove his hat and nod to Mrs. Ward, who'd immediately called out a hello to him. His journey across the diner was slow, as almost every person he passed greeted him, asking how he was doing. The entire town loved Hal Jenkins.

All eyes followed Hal as he headed for the booth where Lucy waited and slid in opposite her. No one openly put their heads together to talk, but many knowing glances were exchanged.

Lucy slid a menu to Hal. "Everything all right?"

Hal brushed the menu aside, asked for iced tea from the waitress who'd followed him over, and rested his arms on the table.

"I told Ross everything," he said, once the waitress had

gone. "Best way. He knew some of it from the police records, but I filled in the rest."

"The fact that you're here means he didn't immediately lock you in chains." Lucy took a nonchalant sip of her latte, pretending she hadn't been concerned.

"No chains yet," Hal said. "He did tell me not to leave River County."

"Good thing your job isn't over the county line." Lucy lowered her cup. "Did he tell you what happened? Fair warning: I'm nosy and want to know."

Hal had to pause again as the waitress brought the iced tea and asked to take their order. Hal asked for pancakes with a side of sausage and eggs and plenty of hot sauce. Being called in by the sheriff obviously hadn't curbed his appetite.

Lucy ordered a salad for herself, ready for lunch, and the waitress wafted off.

"Ross didn't give me much more information than what he told me on the phone," Hal continued. "Apparently the Campbells and Jack are in the clear, which just leaves me."

"If you'd been fighting, your hands would be all bruised." Lucy reached across the table and ran her fingers over Hal's tanned and callused, but injury-free, knuckles.

Hal closed his fingers to trap hers within his. Lucy pressed her lips together to keep from beaming an elated smile.

Her intimacy with him was new, and its imprint hadn't left her. She could still feel Hal's body against hers, his kisses, his touch like fire.

Hal flushed, telling Lucy he was thinking of their encounter as well. Nate's situation and Ross's questioning hadn't killed the fresh excitement of it.

"I don't think Ross believes I did it," Hal said. "But he doesn't know who did. I don't like the idea that there's someone out there who could take down a man as nasty as Redfern."

He closed both hands over Lucy's as he finished the statement. Lucy drew a breath, amazed at how the rest of the world faded when she was with him.

"Ross will find out," she made herself say. "He's smart."

"Hope so." Hal's expression darkened.

Lucy squeezed his hands in return. "At least you have an alibi, right? You'd already gone home by the time I left the bar, right?" She remembered how Hal had quit the place after Lucy had asked him to dance—she understood now he'd been worried about Redfern and hadn't wanted to explain every detail in the middle of the bar. "You go home every night and sleep hard, because you work all the time. Everyone knows that."

Hal's flush deepened. "Yeah, well ..."

Lucy's brows rose. "Wait, you didn't go home?"

"No."

At that inconvenient moment, their food arrived—suspiciously fast for such a busy restaurant.

Lucy thanked the waitress, who gave them a frankly curious stare as she asked if they needed anything else. Once she'd finally departed, Lucy took up her fork and picked at the arugula and kale in her salad.

She hoped Hal would begin explaining where he'd gone last night, but Hal only slopped hot sauce over his eggs and syrup onto his pancakes. He concentrated on this task as though it was the most important thing ever.

Once Hal had his food coated to his liking, he took a large bite in silence. Lucy crunched a sliver of carrot while she waited.

Hal wasn't going to answer, she realized as time passed. *That's what I get for falling for a man of few words.*

"You don't have to tell me," Lucy said. She left the rest of the thought hanging: *But I wish you would.*

Hal glanced up from his food, as though surprised Lucy hadn't moved on to another topic. "There was something I had to do." By the chagrin in his eyes, it had been something embarrassing. "I wasn't with a woman, or anything like that," Hal added quickly. "Or beating up Redfern."

"Well, whew." Lucy wiped her hand across her forehead. "I worried you'd gone to that swinger orgy in White Fork." She relented as Hal's brows rose in startled shock. "I'm kidding. There was no swinger orgy in White Fork ...well, as far as I know, anyway."

"We could ask Karen," Hal said, his expression neutral.

Lucy burst out laughing in genuine mirth. Yes, anything kinky in River County would be on Karen's radar. "You always come up with a good one."

Hal shrugged, returning to his food. "I got a million of 'em."

If Hal did have a million one-liners, he kept them buried deep inside himself. Every once in a while he'd let out a zinger, surprising any listener that he actually had a sense of humor.

"Still waters run deep," Lucy quoted.

"That's what I hear."

One thing Lucy liked about Hal was that he didn't leap into every conversation with a loud opinion or try to dominate those around him. He could be forceful when necessary, but he didn't yell and rant or try to be overly funny and annoying. He was a peaceful man to be with but never boring.

It was also clear he wasn't going to tell her what he'd been up to last night. Any further questions would sound like nagging.

Whatever Hal had been doing was his own business, right? Lucy told herself. It wasn't as though they were a couple.

"So," Lucy said after a few bites of salad. "Should we talk about the elephant in the room?"

"Shit." Hal dropped his fork and glanced around in amazement. "There's an elephant in the diner?"

"Damn it." Lucy laughed again, abandoning all pretense of eating. "No wonder I like you."

Hal's teasing fell away in an instant. He reached for his iced tea, his hand shaking. He lifted the glass but didn't drink, then cleared his throat.

"That's nice of you to say," he said, so softly that Lucy barely caught the words.

"I wasn't being nice. It's the truth." Lucy leaned to him, letting her voice reach him alone. "What we did at your house was terrific."

Hal continued to blush, but a wicked sparkle entered his eyes. "Yeah, I thought so too."

They regarded each other in silence, while around them, the diner rang with conversation and laughter, kids shrieking for parents' attention, and Mrs. Ward yelling an order into the kitchen. In the booth, a bubble of quiet understanding settled over Hal and Lucy, one that belied the elation in Lucy's heart.

Hal cleared his throat again. "Should we maybe, um, do it again sometime?"

"Yes," Lucy answered breathlessly. "I'd like that."

"Maybe dinner first? Next Saturday night? After the rodeo." Even the tips of Hal's ears were red.

"Sure." Lucy hoped she didn't sound inane. "That's fine with me."

"Okay then."

"Okay."

Food forgotten, the two studied each other, neither wanting to look away.

"Jenkins!" A loud, jovial voice cut through Lucy's contemplation of Hal's fine brown eyes. "Are you—oops. Sorry."

A burly man with shaggy brown hair and a hard body halted next to the booth. Behind him were two other men, both taller and leaner than the first. These men had sand-colored hair and identical light blue eyes that scanned first Hal then Lucy and began sparkling in delight.

Lucy recognized them. They were rodeo clowns—Martin, who'd yelled Hal's name, and the Gaskell brothers, whom Lucy had known since high school.

"Looks like we're interrupting a date," Martin went on in his booming voice. The brothers, quieter by nature, only smiled hard.

Lucy expected Hal to jerk away and deny he and Lucy were even sitting at the same table, but Hal reached across and squeezed her fingers.

"Not a date this time," he said to his friends. "Just having some lunch."

"Hey, Lucy," Martin nodded at her. The brothers followed suit.

"Hey, yourself." Lucy barely knew what she said, her heart full with Hal's hand securing hers. "How's it going, Abel? Jesse?"

The Gaskell brothers, never ones for speaking much, responded with "not bad," and "okay."

"Really sorry we interrupted," Martin said. "I didn't see you, Lucy. There's the meeting today, Hal, and I thought I'd remind you."

"Oh." Hal struggled to hide his dismay, but Martin and the others didn't seem to notice. "I did forget. Rodeo clown meet-up," Hal told Lucy. "We're getting ready for the season. I have to be there."

"That's okay." Lucy had hoped they'd return to Hal's place and finish what they'd started, but life was good at interfering with amorous activities. "You guys truly run the rodeo. We need you."

Hal had saved her brother's butt not long ago when Kyle had taken a very bad fall that had put him out for the season. Lucy had been in Houston then, but Anna had told her the story in great detail. Anna had been doing a stint as a rodeo clown herself that day.

"Mind giving me a lift?" Hal asked Martin. "My truck's at home."

Martin switched his gaze to Lucy again, his interest in the situation growing. "Sure thing."

Lucy drew a breath to say she could drive Hal—she'd love another half hour in his company—but she subsided. Hal might prefer to arrive at the rodeo grounds with his friends than be dropped off by his ...well, whatever Lucy was to him.

"Be with you in a bit," Hal said pointedly to Martin.

"What? Oh." Martin started, then made it obvious he got the hint. He raised his hands as he backed away, gave Lucy an exaggerated wink, and then turned around and shooed Jesse and Abel from the table. The Gaskell brothers beamed in delight and followed Martin back through the restaurant.

"Go ahead," Lucy said when Hal lifted his glass to slowly sip his tea. "I'll take care of the check."

Hal lowered his glass again. "The hell you will. This might not be a real date, but I'm not running out on a woman and leaving her to pick up the tab. My folks taught me better than that."

Lucy relaxed. "I won't argue."

His old-fashioned courtesy warmed her. Hal took his time finishing his breakfast and iced tea, waiting until Lucy had eaten her fill of the salad. By tacit agreement, they didn't mention Nate Redfern or Ross. They spoke mostly about mutual friends and what was going on with them, and the pool Mrs. Kaye had started about the gender of Anna's baby.

"I already put twenty on girl," Hal said.

"Why is that your guess?" Lucy asked.

"I don't know, really." Hal shrugged. "But she'll drive Kyle crazy, and it's worth a twenty to think about that."

Lucy laughed. This morning she'd laughed more than she had all year, and it felt good.

When she finally walked out of the diner with Hal—every head craned to watch them go—Lucy's heart was light. Martin and the Gaskells were waiting at a large pickup not far into the lot, and Martin waved when he saw Hal.

Lucy didn't think Hal would kiss her good-bye, and he didn't. He clasped her hands and gave her a little smile.

That was a rare thing for Hal Jenkins. Lucy held that smile to herself, letting it fill up the empty spaces as he made his way to Martin and climbed into the front seat of the man's pickup.

Hal waved at Lucy as they pulled out, and she waved back. The world that had been rocking for the past year was suddenly solid beneath her feet.

———

LUCY DROVE THE FEW BLOCKS HOME AND PARKED HER CAR in front of her house. Mrs. Kaye was in her garden, working hard to get it ready for summer. It would be a gorgeous riot of blooms by May.

"Did you see Hal?" Mrs. Kaye asked her without a greeting. "I heard Ross arrested him for beating up a man who bothered him in the bar. What do you know about that?"

CHAPTER TEN

Lucy paused with one foot on her porch step. "News travels fast."

"This is Riverbend," Mrs. Kaye said in a reasonable tone. "Everyone saw Hal go into the sheriff's office this morning, and it's all over town about the young man half-dead up at the medical clinic."

Lucy turned from her house, her voice going hard. "Then everyone would have seen Hal come back out of the sheriff's office. Ross wanted to ask him a few questions because Hal knew the guy, that's all. Then Hal had breakfast with me."

"Now, don't get riled, Lucy Malory." Mrs. Kaye straightened up from her flower bed, her gloves and trowel covered with dark earth. "I've been out here all morning and am only repeating what six people said to me as they went by."

"Hal had nothing to do with it. That's what he says, and I believe him. Ross believes him too." Lucy reined in her temper. There was no reason to get mad at Mrs. Kaye for revealing what others were speculating. "I wish Hal would tell Ross where he was last night. Hal said there was something he had to do, but he didn't elaborate on what."

"Oh, I wouldn't worry about that." Mrs. Kaye spoke with great confidence. "Hal's a nice boy. He was probably helping out a friend, or rescuing kittens, or some such thing. He wouldn't have had time to find a man and beat him up—not that he even would."

Mrs. Kaye's stout defense of Hal made Lucy ashamed of her need to know what Hal had been up to. "You're right," she said, trying to echo Mrs. Kaye's tone. "Whatever Hal was doing it's his business, and he probably was helping someone. I'll bet he doesn't want to say, to protect whoever it was from gossip."

That would be far more in character for Hal than putting a man in the hospital and then denying he did it. If Hal had fought with Nate, he'd have owned up to it—would likely be sitting by Nate's bedside even now to make sure he'd be okay.

Lucy was a little hurt Hal wouldn't trust her with the details of his errand, though she supposed it was too soon for that. They'd had a morning of steaming hotness in his living room, yes, but that was no reason for Hal to suddenly confide all his secrets to her.

Lucy wondered then—how *had* Nate reached the hospital? A good Samaritan? Had Nate managed to stagger to the ER on his own? Or had his attacker dumped him at the door? Ross must have thought of this too and would even now be investigating.

"I hope Ross finds out who did it," Lucy said to Mrs. Kaye, who was watching her closely. "Ross believes Hal—or at least Hal thinks he does—but Ross is careful."

"Ross is also a smart boy. I'm sure it will all work out in the end."

"I hope so." Lucy resumed her journey up her porch steps. "Thanks, Mrs. Kaye."

"Always a pleasure talking with you, Lucy."

Lucy reached her front door and let herself inside. She caught a glimpse of Mrs. Kaye, who studied Lucy with a thoughtful expression. Lucy closed the door, her thoughts immediately returning to Hal and his kisses, which wiped out any speculations as to why Mrs. Kaye wore such a knowing look.

———

HAL'S MEETING AT THE RODEO GROUNDS WAS PRETTY standard—they went over the schedule of upcoming events, figured out how many people they'd need at each, and who was doing what, when. Hal would work this coming Saturday morning and afternoon, with Martin and the Gaskells, among others, taking over in the evening. The schedule suited Hal, giving him time to clean up and take Lucy to dinner.

He'd also carved out the day of the Bluebonnet Festival for himself. He wasn't certain about asking Lucy yet—he'd wait and see how this upcoming date went first. But just in case ...

During the meeting, Martin told everyone he'd seen Hal with Lucy at the diner, holding hands.

There followed a roomful of laughter and teasing. Hal didn't mind their ribbing—as long as they kept anything they said about Lucy clean and polite. They tried to pry out of him how far Hal and Lucy had gone, but they didn't succeed. Hal didn't kiss and tell.

Martin drove Hal home after the meeting, continuing to prod him for information during the ride, both about Lucy and

Redfern. Hal gave very limited answers regarding either and Martin had to drive away after he dropped Hal off, unsatisfied.

Hal entered his house and sank to the couch, not even bothering to head for the kitchen for something to wet his throat. He eyed the chair where he and Lucy had gone pretty far, recalling Lucy's supple body beneath his hands, the silken skin of her breasts, the sounds she made in her throat as he'd pleasured her.

He didn't get much done the rest of that afternoon.

She'd agreed to go out with him—that fact made Hal's legs shaky whenever he thought of it—but that wouldn't be until next Saturday. A whole week away.

A whole week of him thinking about Lucy and trying not to anticipate that the date would go bad.

Ross hadn't un-invited him from the cookout this evening, but Hal decided to skip it. Even though Ross had said Hal was still welcome, he didn't feel right about going, not until Ross figured out who'd actually assaulted Redfern. There would be some awkwardness, and Hal wasn't ready to face that.

At eight, Hal gave up trying to do anything productive around the house and headed to town to the bar. River County wasn't dry, but there were local liquor laws, so the bar opened at noon on Sunday and closed at a modest eleven p.m.

Many people had decided to meet friends and family on this Sunday night, but there was one notable absence.

"Lucy isn't here," Rosa informed Hal as she set a bottle of his favorite beer on the counter.

"Am I that obvious?" Hal asked in resignation as he took up the bottle.

Rosa flashed a grin. "Only to me, honey. She's at the Campbells' place for a family dinner."

That had figured into Hal's debate whether or not to go.

Ever since Lucy's sister Grace had married into the Campbell family, the Campbells and the Malorys had put aside their rivalry and welcomed each other into their family homes.

Mostly put aside the rivalry. Neither set of brothers was willing to yield superiority to the other. Their encounters made for some entertainment for the rest of town.

As much as he wanted to see Lucy, Hal still couldn't bring himself to drive out to Circle C Ranch and barge in, asking for some barbecue.

He lingered on his barstool, watching friends and family converse and couples dance, nodding to those who greeted him.

"At least you're not in custody." Jack Hillman landed next to Hal, his inked arms bared by a short-sleeved T-shirt.

"Nope." Hal saw no reason to expound.

Jack already had a beer and took a sip. "I heard about Redfern's injuries, in some detail." Jack knew everyone, and he probably had a friend who worked at the medical center. "Not your M.O. The few times I've seen you fight, you take your opponent down fast and then leave him catching his breath and thinking over what he just learned. This attack was vicious. Lots of anger in it. That isn't you."

"I can get plenty mad." Hal had in the past, which was another reason he'd given up the rodeo circuit.

Jack shook his head. "Not like this. If whoever did it wasn't trying to kill Redfern, they wanted him to be afraid of them."

"I'm thinking maybe some of his old friends," Hal said. "Well, not friends. Co-workers. Could be that Redfern didn't spend as much time in prison as they thought he should."

"Co-workers." Jack chuckled softly. "A good term. If they did this, they sound like some evil guys."

"They were." Hal cooled his fingers on his bottle's droplet-filmed glass. "Redfern and his crew were making money, and they weren't going to let anyone get in the way of it. Not me, not law enforcement, not animal rights people. Redfern and his dad had a lot of people paid off."

"Which helped Redfern get out of prison faster, I'd bet," Jack concluded. "And those who took most of the blame could be seeking revenge."

"If any of them are out," Hal said. "I don't know—I walked away and left it all behind me."

"Yeah, I can appreciate that." Jack took a long swallow of his beer.

Jack never talked about his past and the things he'd done, and Hal didn't ask. If Jack had wanted to talk about it, he already would have. Both Hal and Jack had made the decision to settle down and have as normal a life as possible, letting their pasts remain in the rearview mirror.

"Ross must already know all this," Hal said. "He's thorough."

"He is. But he's also a decent guy. I don't know if he can wrap his head around this kind of shit." Jack paused for a thoughtful moment. "If you want, I'll find out if Redfern's old gang have been sprung. I, for one, don't want them around if they have been. I can make sure they leave River County alone."

"Better not," Hal warned. "They're dangerous. Doping cattle isn't their only activity, just one that they found lucrative for a while. I know them. Let me deal with it."

Jack shook his head. "They'll try to hurt you, like they did Redfern. Me, they *don't* know, and they won't understand what hit them until it's too late." His smile did not bode well for any who got in his way.

"These guys aren't messing around, Jack," Hal said.

"Neither am I." Jack's smile softened into something genuine. "But hey, if they come after you, you'll have Lucy to kiss it all better."

Hal didn't laugh, though his blood tingled at the thought of Lucy's mouth anywhere on his body. "Never say that in front of her brothers," he said. "I'm serious."

"I hear you, man." Jack thunked his bottle to the bar. "A while back, before Grace hooked up with Carter, I thought about taking her out." His eyes flickered. "Ray swiftly disabused me of that notion."

Hal could imagine what Ray's reaction had been. Even Jack would back away from the large and rumbling Ray Malory when Ray was unhappy. "He and Kyle are very protective of their sisters," Hal said in commiseration.

"Too true. It didn't matter in my case, though. Grace never would have looked at me. With her, it was always Carter."

Hal agreed. Grace was madly in love with Carter Sullivan, and she'd never pretended not to be, no matter how many people had warned her against him. Now she was happily married to him, and the two were raising their cute kids.

"I don't blame Kyle and Ray," Jack continued. "Their sisters are great ladies. I'm protective of them now too." Jack looked Hal straight in the eye, and Hal instantly understood why Jack was highly respected by thugs and honest men alike. "Don't hurt Lucy."

Hal returned his gaze without flinching. "I never would."

Whatever Jack saw in Hal's expression satisfied him. He lifted his beer, and the men clinked bottles in a toast to the Malory sisters, two of the best women in Riverbend.

———

Lucy spent her supper with the Campbells edgy. While Ross had invited Hal, he wasn't here, and she couldn't help constantly watching out for him. She tried to enjoy Grace's brilliant cooking, Grant's stellar chili, and Ross's skill at the grill, but her thoughts returned again and again to Hal.

Because of the crowd—five Campbell brothers and their wives, Malory brothers and *their* wives, assorted kids, and Olivia Campbell, the proud mom and grandma, radiant due to her newfound love with Sam Farrell—they ate at picnic tables on the porch and in the yard, the evening air pleasant.

Lucy cornered Ross as she walked up to him for seconds of his barbecued chicken. Anna hadn't quite convinced Lucy to be vegan yet.

"Hal didn't do it," Lucy said.

Ross jerked the fork he was using to turn over ribs on one side of the grill. A piece fell to the grating, splashing hot grease over Ross's full-length apron.

"Way to be subtle, Luce."

Ross turned the ribs more carefully. With a long fork, he chose a seared chicken breast and set the meat on her plate.

"Only way to get you to talk about it," Lucy said. The whole evening, everyone had carefully avoided the topic of Hal. "He did not assault Nate. I guarantee it."

"I don't think he did either, but the town police in White Fork are eyeballing him. Would help a lot if he'd tell me exactly where he was." Ross gave Lucy a steady look.

She raised a hand, balancing her plate in the other. "Don't glare at me. I don't know."

"You could convince him to tell *me*."

Lucy's brows went up. "What makes you think he'll listen to me? Hal already told me he'd had business to take care of—

not beating up Nate business. I believe him," she finished stoutly.

Ross shook his head and went back to expertly turning meat. Anything Ross cooked was perfectly done without being dried out.

"I'm trying to keep him out of jail, all right? Talk to him?" Ross sent her the appealing glance he'd learned at a very young age, which made everyone, particularly women and girls, drop everything to do whatever Ross Campbell wanted.

Lucy found herself nodding. "I don't know if I'll run into him again before Saturday, but okay."

"I'll bet you run into him sooner than you think. Just ask? Thank you, Lucy."

This man had River County wrapped around his handsome little finger. No wonder Callie Jones, daughter of the richest man in River County, had fallen hopelessly in love with him.

"Sure thing, Ross."

Lucy walked away with her chicken, wondering how it happened that she'd gone to interrogate Ross and left promising to do him a favor.

This was why her brothers had told her when she was little to never trust a Campbell.

Kyle and Ray were right now laughing uproariously at some joke with Tyler, Adam, and Grant Campbell, the collective Malory and Campbell kids playing together in the grass. How times had changed.

For the better, Lucy decided, and settled down to enjoy her delicious meal.

———

"You're in early," Dr. Anna remarked as she entered the vet's office the next morning, Lucy already at her desk.

Lucy didn't look up from her spreadsheet. She liked spreadsheets, which neatly logged every detail she needed and could add up numbers with the click of a mouse. There was more dedicated accounting software out there, but there was something satisfying about the control Lucy had on a spreadsheet.

"It's Monday," Lucy responded. "Time for work."

There would be a lot to do, getting ready for the fast-approaching day Anna would go on maternity leave. Dr. Calvert, a vet from Llano and an old friend of Anna's, was taking over for her during her absence, and Lucy needed to make sure she had all the information to give him at her fingertips.

Anna stared at Lucy until she lifted her head, then Anna's puzzled expression gave way to a wise understanding and some amusement.

Lucy's eyes narrowed. "What? Was everyone laughing at me once I left last night?"

She'd departed Circle C Ranch soon after the meal ended, saying she was tired and of course had work the next morning. Anna and Kyle had stayed behind, deep in conversation with Grace and family.

"No." Anna leaned her hands on Lucy's desk. "Something Margaret told us when she came in this morning."

Margaret was the savvy woman who managed the Malory ranch's office. She'd started working there while Lucy had been living in Houston, and Lucy had come to know that Margaret was smart, capable, and good at putting up with her brothers' bullshit.

"I can see you're dying to tell me," Lucy said tiredly. "What did Margaret say?"

Anna peered hard at Lucy, searching for ... what? "She told me that she knows exactly where Hal Jenkins was when he was supposedly beating up his old enemy."

"Oh?" Lucy tried not to sound interested. She wasn't sure how reliable this information would be—how would Margaret know when Hal wasn't about to tell Ross or Lucy?

Anna leaned closer, as much as her round belly would let her. "He was with you, sis-in-law." She winked. "I think we all know doing what."

CHAPTER ELEVEN

L ucy opened her mouth to instantly deny that Hal had been anywhere near her after he'd left the bar Saturday night, but slowly closed it.

Whoever had started the rumor likely did because no one actually knew where Hal had been. Some joker must have decided to speculate that Hal went to Lucy's that night and stayed there, and the story had spread.

Better that than Hal was out beating someone down, wasn't it?

Lucy felt herself blush. Even though the tale was untrue, she could vividly picture snuggling against Hal's broad shoulder in his or her bed after a round of fantastic sex. He'd draw her to him, kiss her hair, whisper something that made her blood heat. Coupled with what they'd done yesterday, her imagination was creative indeed.

Anna laughed in delight. "Damn, Lucy. Why didn't you tell me?"

Lucy attempted a mysterious expression. "I haven't had

the chance, have I? Anyway, it's personal. Between Hal and me."

"I'm sure it is. Well, I won't talk about it if you don't want to."

"I don't. Thank you."

Anna was usually the last person who liked to chatter about other people's relationships, but Lucy could tell she was disappointed she couldn't learn more. Anna tamped down her curiosity as she rose to return to business.

"Well, if you ever want to ..." She left it open, and Lucy nodded.

"Thanks, Anna."

"Any time." Anna made her way through the door to the surgical suites, where she needed to prep for her first patient, leaving Lucy to herself.

Anna hadn't questioned the truth of the rumor. It was interesting that all Lucy had to do was smile and flush, and she'd convey she'd been hot and heavy with Hal all Saturday night.

Her amusement fled when she realized that Hal would also hear the rumor. He couldn't not. Hal was painfully honest, and he would argue long and hard that the story wasn't true. No one would believe him, of course, but that wasn't the problem.

What if Hal grew angry that the whole town was talking about him rolling in the hay with Lucy? Whether they had or hadn't? Would that embarrassment make him want to never see Lucy again? He might even believe *she'd* started the rumor in an attempt to protect him.

Lucy raked her cell phone from her purse and called him.

No answer. Hal's pleasant baritone rumbled to her as he

explained he couldn't answer right now, but to leave a voice mail.

"Hal. It's Lucy. We need to talk."

Lucy winced as she ended the call. The four words no guy wanted to hear, and she'd said them without explanation.

Oh, well. If Hal didn't respond, she'd figure out how to get word to him somehow. She could text him or she could leave another voice mail, this one longer, though she wasn't quite certain yet what she was going to say. Easier to speak to him directly.

No matter how Hal felt about it, he'd bend over backward to prove he was anywhere but in Lucy's bed, which might get him arrested if he'd simply been in the wrong place at the wrong time that night.

Crap on a crutch. Life was getting complicated.

Lucy's thoughts cut off when the door opened to admit the first patient of the day. Mrs. Barton, a friend of Mrs. Kaye, carried in a small dog crate covered by a thin blanket. Lucy checked her screen—8:15, *Belle, dachshund, eye discharge*—and pulled up the dog's record.

"Good morning, Mrs. Barton," Lucy said as soon as the woman stepped inside.

"Good morning, Lucy." Mrs. Barton paused to smooth her short, windblown curls, then sent Lucy a wise look. "You and Hal should be careful, you know, or you'll be a mommy and daddy before you realize. I know you young people don't care whether you're married or not anymore, but at least make sure you're a couple with an understanding first. A child needs its parents to be there for them."

Lucy didn't think her face could grow any hotter. "Jumping the gun a little, Mrs. Barton."

"You used protection? Oh, that's good."

Thankfully, Anna opened the door at that moment and called Mrs. Barton inside. Mrs. Barton waved at Lucy and lugged her dachshund toward the examination room. The dog whined, knowing damn well where it was, despite the shielding blanket. Mrs. Barton began to chatter to Anna about her poor dog's afflictions, and the door shut.

"Shit." Lucy said the word out loud and pressed her palms to her eyes. "I hope to hell the entire county isn't wondering when we'll expect our first kid. Or whether we used protection. *Damn* it."

She could nip this whole thing in the bud by marching into the exam room—okay, waiting until the dog was taken care of—and explaining to Anna and Mrs. Barton that the whole thing had been made up. She hadn't had sex with Hal, not Saturday night, not ever.

Lucy rehearsed the speech in her head, setting up a debate like the best courtroom lawyer, then she deflated.

It wouldn't matter. People believed what they wanted. The story that Hal refused to tell Ross where he was to protect Lucy's reputation was a better one than the truth, whatever that was. Much more romantic. Everyone loved a good romantic tale.

Lucy let out a muffled groan. The train she'd climbed aboard was careening out of control, fast.

———

DUSTY AND TIRED AFTER A LONG DAY OFFLOADING twenty head of new cattle, separating them into corrals, and looking them over to make sure they were sound, Hal made his way to Riverbend's diner for a bite.

He often headed there after work, no one minding that he smelled of cow in his corner booth by the open back door.

Today, after Mrs. Ward's oldest daughter had brought him his chicken-fried steak and extra mashed potatoes, Hal glanced up to see Kyle and Ray Malory slip into the booth to face him over the table.

"Hey." Hal greeted the two collectively and went back to eating, hungry. He hadn't had time for lunch.

"Hey, yourself," Kyle said. "Something you want to tell us, Jenkins?"

Hal's loaded fork paused on the way to his mouth. Kyle was glaring at him with hard green eyes. Ray said nothing and he didn't glare, but Ray could be intimidating just by sitting there.

"About ...?" Hal took the bite, pretending the two Malory brothers ganging up on him didn't unnerve him.

"You and Lucy," Kyle said.

Hal started to cough, swallowed, and wiped his mouth on a large paper napkin. "What about me and Lucy?" There was no *me and Lucy* as of yet. Only in Hal's dreams.

Kyle rested his arms on the table and leaned in. "We like you, Jenkins. But Lucy went through some bad shit with her last boyfriend."

"Clyde." Hal gave him a slow nod. "I know. I hate that dickhead."

Kyle's expression softened somewhat. "Yeah, I'd like to find him and explain a few things. But Lucy would have my ass for it."

Ray rumbled something in his throat. The sound was very soft but drew Hal's attention, as Ray intended. "We don't want to see Lucy hurt again," Ray stated flatly.

Hal laid down his knife and fork, pushing his tasty meal aside for the moment.

"I want to explain something to you," he said, meeting both men's gazes. "The last thing in the world I'm willing to do is hurt Lucy. I never would. Whatever kind of relationship she figures she'll have with me is up to her. I'm not pushing for anything she doesn't want."

Hal thought this summed things up well, but for some reason, Ray and Kyle both looked more pissed off than before.

"What exactly are you saying?" Kyle demanded. "That what you have with her is only casual?"

Hal maintained his even tone. "What I'm saying is it's not up to me. I really like Lucy. But I'm not going to drag her into a relationship and then break her heart. If she wants casual, then that's what it will be."

Ray bent closer, like a threatening thundercloud. "It's not just about what she wants," Ray declared. "It's also about her reputation. I don't want it all over town she's out for casual anything."

Hal sent him a baffled look. Before he could ask what the hell Ray was implying, an angry shadow fell over all three men.

Hal turned to see Lucy, beautiful and fuming, hands on hips, scowling at Kyle and Ray.

"Are you two finished?" she demanded.

Kyle went red. "Hey, Lucy. We were just—"

"Oh, I know what you were doing. Interfering in my life like the pain-in-the-ass brothers you are."

Ray flushed guiltily, though he tried to brazen through. "We're just looking out for you, Lu."

Lucy's eyes filled with rage. "I'm a grown-ass woman, Ray Malory. Save your over-protectiveness for your own kids, the poor things. I'll tell them they'll have a refuge at Aunt Lucy's."

"Lucy, come on," Kyle began.

"Don't *come on* me. My relationship with Hal is none of your damned business, either of you. He's a wonderful guy—point out a better one in this town. Which you can't. There isn't one thing you can object to in Hal, so back off. Whatever we decide we want is up to us, not *you*. Whether we become a thing or go our separate ways, it's *our* choice."

Hal lifted his cup of coffee during her diatribe and took a satisfied sip, trying not to wallow in the joy of Lucy calling him *wonderful*. And was there a chance of them becoming a thing? This was turning into a great day.

The Malory brothers did not like being told off by their little sister, especially not in front of the very full diner. Even Mrs. Ward and her daughters had paused in their rush to listen.

"I appreciate your concern," Hal told Kyle and Ray before they could resume the argument. "I share it. But why don't you let Lucy and me talk by ourselves?"

Hal had no anger in his voice, only friendly firmness. Lucy, however, wasn't finished.

"Yes, please go home to your wives who are waiting for you. How about I text them and let them know what you've been up to?" Lucy slid her phone from a pocket in her purse and let her thumbs hover over the screen. "I'm sure they'll be thrilled."

Ray, who sat on the inside of the booth, pushed Kyle. "Nope. Move it, Kyle, we're going."

Kyle heaved a sigh as he pried himself up. He towered over Lucy, but she only frowned at him, thumbs at the ready.

"Out," Lucy told him.

"Come on." Ray, now on his feet and taller than his brother, turned Kyle around by the shoulders. "See you, Lu. Hal."

Lucy waited without speaking, her expression so obstinate that Hal wanted to laugh. Lucy was diminutive next to her hulking brothers, but she had them hurrying away home without breaking a sweat.

She remained ready to text until Kyle and Ray walked out of the diner, Ray tipping his hat at those who'd chosen to applaud as they departed. The brothers separated to climb into their respective pickups and drive quickly away.

Only then did Lucy drop her phone into her purse and slide in across from Hal.

Hal preferred the sister to the brothers. Lucy's cheeks were pink, her green eyes sparkling, her curves complemented by a soft blouse and thin necklace against her throat.

"I should text Drew and Anna anyway." Lucy broke into a smile, which made her all the more beautiful. "I can only yell at Kyle and Ray when I see them, but their wives can keep at it all night." She laughed, and then waved to a hurrying waitress for an iced tea.

"I like this," Hal said after the tea landed in front of Lucy. "You running to my rescue." He also enjoyed watching Lucy's red lips close around the straw, which made him think of things Kyle and Ray would definitely kill him for.

"My brothers can be a pain in my ass." Lucy's smile vanished. "Have been my entire life. If I embarrass them in the diner, they deserve it."

"They're worried about you," Hal said. "I understand why. They don't want to see you hurt again." He let his voice be gentle. "I don't either."

His statements brought back Lucy's laughter, to his

surprise. "They didn't gang up on you because they're afraid you're another Clyde," she informed him. "They barged in here and cornered you because someone started the rumor that we're sleeping together, and it's all over town. In fact, that's where you were Saturday night, so they say. In my bed, instead of out beating up Nate Redfern."

CHAPTER TWELVE

H al sprayed half the mouthful of coffee he'd taken over the table and choked on the other half.

Lucy jerked napkins from the dispenser and handed them to him. Hal took them in shaky fingers and wiped off his face as Lucy scrubbed the table.

Holy fucking shit. No wonder Ray and Kyle had hovered as though they wanted to lunge across the table and throttle Hal. They thought he'd slept with their baby sister, and here he was calmly eating chicken-fried steak.

"I'm sorry," Hal said when he could speak. "I don't know who would say that about you. I'll find them and ... have a talk with them."

Lucy laced her fingers together and rested her chin on them, elbows on the table. "Don't bother. I don't mind."

Hal stared at her. "You don't?"

"No. Why should I? Look at them all." Lucy glanced sideways at the diners trying to pretend they weren't watching Hal and Lucy. "I'm getting laid by the sexiest cowboy in town, and they're eating their hearts out."

Emotions tumbled through Hal's brain. First, wonder that Lucy wasn't upset or offended. Second, amazement at Lucy's description of him. Third, a hungry need to make the rumors fact, one that blotted out his other thoughts.

"Sexiest cowboy in town, huh?" Hal attempted a light tone. "It's a pretty small town."

Lucy shrugged her shoulders, which made the gold chain move across her throat. "Sexiest in the state, then. It's a pretty big state. Well populated."

Hal tried to tamp down his glee. "You really don't mind people saying we're ..." He opened one hand. "You know."

"Doing the horizontal tango?" Lucy's good humor returned. "Let them. It will keep Ross off your back. Plus, everyone will say what a gentleman you are because you'd rather go to jail than soil my reputation."

"Hmm." Was his freedom worth people talking far and wide about Lucy? She seemed to think so, but Hal didn't agree.

"I didn't mean for my brothers to fly off the handle," Lucy said. "I called to warn you what folks were saying. I should have left a better message, but today's been crazy."

Hal pulled his phone from the pocket of his light jacket. He'd been thrilled that Lucy had spontaneously called him, though he hadn't yet had a chance to return it.

"Yeah, sorry about that," he said. "I was dealing with twenty ornery steers all day. I was going to call you back as soon as I finished eating. Was this what you wanted to talk about?"

Lucy flushed. "I imagined you cringing when I said *we needed to talk* and thought maybe you didn't want to deal with it."

Hal regarded her in puzzlement. "Why should I cringe? I enjoy talking to you."

Lucy stared at him, then she reached across the table to clasp his hands, her face and voice suddenly soft. "Oh, Hal. You've just added another reason to the list of why I like you."

She really shouldn't say things like that, especially not while touching him. Not only did Hal's heart pound, but other parts of his anatomy responded.

"Well, I like you too."

Lucy squeezed his fingers. "Tell you what. I'll order some dinner, and then let's go somewhere and be alone." She leaned closer and murmured, "I'm thinking we should change this rumor into the truth."

She spoke brightly, but Hal saw her brace for his reaction, as though she feared he might spew coffee again.

He closed his hands around hers, his whisper equally quiet, "Maybe we should."

———

LUCY DECIDED THE NIGHT WAS BEAUTIFUL AS SHE WALKED out of the diner. The sun had set in a glory of colors, and stars lit the clearing sky.

She'd had a nice dinner, which she couldn't remember the taste of, and now she was leaving with Hal. She'd gone to the diner on foot—ran there, actually, when she'd seen Kyle and Ray storm inside it when she'd arrived home from work. She'd guessed rightly what they were mad about.

Lucy and Hal had debated about her place or his, and Lucy pointed out his would be much more private. Mrs. Kaye would definitely note Hal coming home with Lucy and inform anyone who walked by of the fact.

Hal expressed concern that his house at the end of the road might be dangerous, in light of Nate's assault, but things had been very quiet in Riverbend since Saturday night. No one had reported anyone hanging around who shouldn't, and no one had threatened Hal.

Plus, Hal had stout locks on his doors. Though River County was safer than most cities, you still had to be cautious these days.

They concluded that privacy was what they needed, and Lucy's body warmed as Hal opened the door of his truck and ushered her inside.

"Hope you don't mind a ride with the windows down," Hal said as they pulled away. "Those steers were not happy about moving to a new ranch."

"Another reason to go to your place." Lucy's window glided down as Hal worked the controls on his side of the car. "I don't have towels big enough for you in my bathroom." She chuckled at Hal's chagrined expression. "You know I have brothers who ride bulls. I'm used to stinky men."

"I guess all the guys you worked with in Houston wore perfume," Hal said. "Excuse me—men's cologne."

"Not all of them." Lucy leaned her arm on the windowsill and enjoyed the clean aroma of the night. "But most of them slathered on scented bath soaps and hair mousse. Had manicures and facials, and never got dirty if they could help it. At first, I was impressed."

"Sounds like a lot of work," Hal said. "My manicure would be done for the minute I had to inoculate a herd." He made a brief show of examining his nails before returning his hand to the steering wheel.

"I got tired of their egos, though. They made fun of Kyle and Ray for being cowboys and bull riders." Lucy had been furious when the firm's sharp-suited men had made her family a running joke. *That your brother texting you? Telling you how much horseshit he ate this morning?*

"I'll bet," Hal said, with feeling.

"The ladies, on the other hand, were intrigued by my brothers." Lucy wrinkled her nose. "They'd ask me if I had pictures of them, naked. 'Cause, yeah, I have nude photos of my brothers on my phone. Creeped me out."

"I, for one, am very glad you don't have naked photos of Kyle and Ray on your phone."

Lucy laughed, loving the moment. Hal Jenkins was next to her on a warm, beautiful spring evening, laying aside his reserve to banter with her.

It was dark by the time Hal turned off onto the long road to his house. The trees whispered in the night, stars peeking through the interlaced leaves.

Hal pulled into his carport and shut down the engine. The sounds of crickets and tree frogs filled the darkness, breaking the immense silence of the outdoors.

Lucy had missed this when she'd lived in the heart of a noisy city—the quietude, the big sky, the serenity of the world just after nightfall. She'd told herself she liked the bustle and excitement, the ability to attend any show or club she wanted, or go to any restaurant with any cuisine she could think of, but her heart had been here in the Hill Country. There was no other place like it.

Even more, she liked following Hal into his home. He checked around for signs of intruders, but Lucy knew they were alone out here. She could feel it. Lights from the house of his nearest neighbor twinkled between the trees, but all else was still.

Hal toed off his boots before he closed his door, tossing them back into the carport.

"I'm going to hit the shower," he said as he locked the door behind him. "Even if I don't use scented soaps and hair gel, I don't want to be smelling like angry cattle all night."

Lucy surveyed him. Maybe once he was all wet and soaped up, she could slide into the bathroom and join him. The thought sent a lovely wave of heat through her.

"First, though." Hal stopped at the entrance to the small hallway and faced her, his cheeks reddening under the glare of the hallway light. "I want to tell you something. If you get mad at me and want to go, I'll drive you back home, no problem. Or —" He fished a car key from his jeans pocket and laid it on the hall table next to him. "You just take my truck. I can grab it next time I'm in town."

Lucy's anticipation ebbed as alarm took over. "What on earth would make me jump into your truck and roar back to town? Do you have a wife and children tucked away in San Angelo? Or are you secretly a spy? Or a gun-running assassin?"

Hal held up a hand to stop her stream of ideas. "Let me tell you. It's about where I really was Saturday night."

Lucy fell silent as a lump formed in her throat. Did he really did have another woman somewhere? That would kick her hard, harder even than what Clyde had done. She really didn't want to have to recover from something like that again.

"Okay." Lucy folded her arms, instinctively closing herself off, though she tried to sound casual. "Where were you after you left the bar Saturday night?"

Hal cleared his throat. "On Mrs. Kaye's front porch."

Lucy's lips parted, but no words escaped them. She stared at Hal, wondering if she'd heard wrong. Of all the things he could have told her, she'd never have dreamed it was that he'd bunked down on Mrs. Kaye's porch.

"I was worried after Redfern started to hit on you at the bar," Hal continued. "I didn't want him following you home and trying to take his revenge on me through you. So, I decided to keep watch on your house. Mrs. Kaye found me, gave me a blanket and pillow, and let me use a chair on her porch. I stayed there until daylight, when I decided it was safe, and came back home."

Lucy's mouth remained partially open as Hal rumbled through his explanation. From the stubborn light in his eyes, he obviously wasn't sorry he'd done it.

"Mrs. Kaye gave you a blanket and pillow," Lucy managed at last. She remembered Mrs. Kaye folding up a blanket on Sunday morning.

"Yep. She didn't want me getting too cold."

"She didn't want you getting too cold." Lucy felt hysterical laughter bubbling inside her and fervently tried to tamp it down. "So, *she* thought it was perfectly fine for you to watch my house all night long."

"Yeah, she did."

Lucy turned away in a daze. She walked through the living room, circled the coffee table, and came back to the hallway.

"Mrs. Kaye was on her porch the next morning," Lucy said slowly. "She never said one word to me about you being there."

"I kind of implied I didn't want her to," Hal said, as though apologizing for her.

"No wonder she looked like she wanted to laugh at me." Lucy glared up at Hal, who regarded her warily. "I bet I know who decided to tell everyone you were sleeping with me that night. I mean, you kind of were—except I was in bed in my house, and you were on my next-door neighbor's porch." The hysterical laughter wanted to become a scream of exasperation.

"So, you're mad at her." Hal traced a line on the wall next to him. "Are you mad at me?"

Lucy remained rigidly silent while emotions whirled through her in a confusing riot.

Anger that neither Mrs. Kaye nor Hal had mentioned that he'd had spent the night on Mrs. Kaye's porch. Feeling like an idiot for not knowing. Irritation that Hal had decided to be so protective of her, just like Ray and Kyle. Also, flooding warmth that Hal had decided to be so protective of her.

Hal hadn't watched over her because he thought he owned her, she realized. He'd done it so that if Nate had followed her home, Hal could intercept him and keep him away from Lucy. Hal wasn't wrong that Nate was dangerous, and that the dickhead might try to use Lucy to get at Hal. He'd been wise to worry. Even if Nate had only tried to coerce Lucy into helping him against Hal, she might have had a tough time getting rid of him.

Nate hadn't come, but if he had, Hal had been there to guard her.

If Ray had done such a thing, Lucy would have yelled at him but also been grateful her tough older brother had been there for her.

"I'm mad at you for not telling me," Lucy said at last. "But not for looking out for me. Thank you."

Hal didn't reach for her, or in any way appear as though he'd clasp her in his arms and declare his devotion, but his eyes softened with understanding.

"I should have said." Hal lowered his hand from the wall. "I'm sorry about that. I didn't tell Ross because I didn't want to drag your name into it. Redfern is my problem. He shouldn't be yours."

Lucy unfolded her arms, wishing Hal would hug her even if he did smell like a herd of cattle. "What a gentleman. Not many like you left."

"Has nothing to do with being a gentleman," Hal said in surprise. "I'm only trying to do what's right. And making a mess of it."

"Not really." Lucy let her voice go quiet. "You go jump in the shower, ranch man. We'll talk some more when you smell like soap instead of cow."

"If you want to leave, I won't blame you." Hal glanced at the key he'd left on the table. "Really."

Lucy gave him a smile. "Take your shower, and we'll see."

Hal lingered a moment then nodded once, as though resigning himself to not knowing her choice, and turned away to the bathroom. The door shut, but he didn't lock it.

Lucy let out a breath as she heard the shower start. "What a sweetie," she whispered.

Most guys she'd known in her life might have demanded her appreciation for watching out for her, most likely with sex. Hal only looked relieved she'd understood. It would never occur to him to ask for anything in return.

Lucy studied the key on the table—an ordinary truck fob on a bit of keychain. Simple, functional, nothing showy.

She left the key where it was and went into the living room to lower the blinds. Same with the kitchen window.

Hal's bedroom at the back of the house was neat. Lucy turned on the lamp on his nightstand and noted that his bed was made, and his clothes had been hung in the closet.

As in the living room, he hadn't placed many photos about. She found one framed picture on his dresser of an older couple, standing on a white sand beach under palm trees. Hal's parents, Lucy concluded. Hal looked very much like his dad. Next to it was a photo of Hal on a bull, the frame resting against a small trophy for one of his rodeo wins.

That was it. No souvenirs, no candid pictures of outings or of Hal lifting beers with friends, brothers, or sisters. Very little from his past.

"Lonely," Lucy murmured into the tidy room. "Like me."

She lowered the blinds in here too. Then she went down the hall to the bathroom and opened the door to plenty of steam.

————

HAL HAD FINISHED RINSING THE SHAMPOO FROM HIS HAIR when the shower door slid open.

He froze, hands at his face to wipe the stream of water from his eyes. Lucy, not wearing a stitch, stepped into the small shower stall with him.

"I decided to come tell you how *not* mad at you I am," she said, before she rose on her tiptoes, put her arms around Hal, and kissed him.

CHAPTER THIRTEEN

H al unfroze. He scooped Lucy to him, her body now wet and warm, and kissed her mouth as she lifted to him.

His world suddenly contained nothing but Lucy against him, her lips seeking. She roved her hands over his body, from the shoulders he'd just soaped, down his back, and to his hips and ass. Not hesitant, she touched him as passionately as she had that morning in his house, but now there was no barrier of clothing between them.

Hal wasn't going to let the phone interrupt this time. He doubted he'd hear it, even if it rang. Lucy's touch had started a roaring in his ears, or maybe that was only the rush of the shower.

Her mouth was hot, her wild kisses like nothing he'd experienced before. The women in his past had either been hesitant with him or hadn't bothered with kissing. Buckle bunnies had usually been in a hurry for the main act with their chosen cowboy.

Lucy, on the other hand, *wanted* to kiss him. She ran fingers through his short hair as she tasted his mouth like she couldn't get enough of him. Hal leaned against the cool tile wall and let her take what she liked.

As much as Hal wanted to seize her and never let go, he made himself gentle his touch. She was worth the gentleness, he thought as he skimmed his fingertips from her hips to the incredible softness of her breasts.

Hal broke the kiss to glide his tongue along her neck, but the compactness of the shower stall prevented him from bending to take her breast in his mouth. He settled for stroking the firm point of her nipple to life, liking it against his fingers.

Lucy wedged her hand to his bottle of bath soap, pumping the dispenser to release a glob liquid from it. She rubbed her palms together to lather up, and then her slick hand went straight to his cock.

"Holy God."

Lucy sent him a mischievous look as she began to stroke him. Hal braced himself on the tile as her fingers danced and played.

His heart hammered, and he screwed his eyes shut tight. Sensations flooded him, fire and pleasure that made him shake.

She couldn't keep going. Lucy had brought him easily to climax when they'd cuddled on the chair in the living room, but water and soapy lubricant was going to release him even faster. There'd be a mess all over Lucy, the shower, and himself.

Hal reached down and tugged Lucy's hand from him.

"Not here," he said in a hoarse whisper. "Bedroom."

Lucy's eyes brightened and she nodded. They both rinsed away the soap, then Hal shut off the water and grabbed a towel.

There was only one in here. Hal hauled it into the stall and wrapped it around Lucy, kissing her while he wiped water from her body.

The towel was soggy by the time Hal had dried off Lucy and she in turn had rubbed him dry. He dumped the towel on the floor, lifted Lucy into his arms, and carried her along the brief hallway to his bedroom.

———

LUCY LANDED ON THE MATTRESS AFTER HAL HAD stripped back the coverings one-handed. The cool bottom sheet met her back, and then Hal joined her. His king-sized bed took up most of the room, but Hal would never fit on a twin. Even a double would be small for him.

Plenty of room for her and Hal together, Lucy decided happily. Hal stretched out next to her, smoothed her hair from her cheek, and kissed her, slowly and leisurely. Neither of them was going anywhere for a while.

Lucy had explored Hal's body in the shower, and now he explored hers. His fingers smoothed her skin from throat, between her breasts, her belly, and to the space between her thighs. He'd brought her to life the other morning, and his touch stirred her once again.

He'd not deflated since the shower, Lucy found when she closed her hand around his cock. Ready and waiting.

They stroked each other a few moments, sounds of pleasure painting the air. Hal ducked his head to take her breast into his mouth, and Lucy's groans grew louder. Nice that they were in a house far from anywhere. She could be as noisy as she liked.

Hal opened the drawer of his nightstand and drew out a box. Unopened, Lucy saw. He struggled with the tab that held it closed, and Lucy, in amusement, ripped it open with her smaller fingers.

They had fun putting the condom on him. As much as she wanted to feel him bare, Lucy appreciated the gesture. She recalled Mrs. Barton at the vet's office radiating approval when she'd decided Lucy and Hal had used protection. Laughter rose within her, but Lucy refused to ruin the moment. She was too hungry for Hal.

Hal kissed her again, once more smoothing her hair back. He was not going to talk dirty to her in bed, she realized. The man of few words wasn't wasting them telling her how hot he was for her. He was showing her instead.

She smiled, loving his silence.

That silence was broken when Hal parted her legs and slid inside her.

"*Damn.*" The word dragged from his throat.

"Like it?" Lucy asked in a whisper, her breath gone.

"Hell, yes."

Lucy glided her hands to his backside. "So do I. Let's keep at it."

Hal's grin and the laughter in his eyes was beautiful to see. Then he closed those eyes, his face softening into pure pleasure as he made his first thrust.

Another groan tore from Lucy's mouth. Hal slowed, as though worried he'd hurt her, but Lucy lifted to him, wrapping one leg around his.

Hal made another thrust, then another, bracing himself to keep his strong body from crushing her. Lucy's mind became a glorious blank, nothing but the sensation of Hal inside her filling the spaces.

Everything hurtful and tiring fell way, all her doubts, fears, and unhappiness since the terrible day her life had changed floating free.

She knew only Hal, his kisses hot on her mouth, his length inside her, stroking her in the best way. He gazed down at her with his heart in his eyes, his longing for her stark. Her longing met his with the same intensity.

The lamplight bathed him in a soft glow, her hard-bodied cowboy damp from the shower, his dark hair sleek with water. Hal's face was the most handsome in the universe, Lucy was certain. His eyes held strength and gentleness at the same time. That was Hal.

He moved faster. Lucy rocked with him. The exhaustion that had haunted her since she'd moved back to Riverbend vanished. She met every thrust with equal fervor, their cries ringing together in the small room.

Outside, wind rattled the windows and fluttered in the trees. Inside, Lucy was safe in Hal's arms, his body bringing hers to life. Lucy cried his name, and many other words besides—whatever they were, she wasn't certain.

Hal's voice finally rocketed out of him, louder than anything she'd heard come from his mouth, and then he was holding her hard, releasing himself deep inside her.

Lucy's own climax hit her, the room darkening as wild sensation poured through her. She loved this, and Hal.

That simple realization smacked her like a blow. Through it, her euphoria flowed on, this coming the most intense she'd experienced in her life.

Hal had given her this gift. She wound herself around him as she came down from her peak, in newfound strength, love, and gratitude.

———

LUCY WAS WIDE AWAKE. NO FALLING INTO POST-COITAL slumber—she was excited and giddy and not ready to sleep.

She rolled over to find Hal smiling at her, his brown eyes warm. She rested her head on his chest, snuggling into his wide and comfortable shoulder. Hal caressed her hair, his touch incredibly tender.

"So, what do we do now?" Hal asked.

Lucy sent him a sly look. "Oh, I can think of all kinds of things we can do."

His brief grin shone out. "I meant about us."

Us? Lucy's heart constricted. *There was an us?* She truly hoped so.

"What about it?" she managed to say.

"It's been a long time since I asked a girl to go steady."

Go steady. He was adorable. People usually said *exclusive* or *casual*, both of which were a step above *hookup*.

"Did you ask girls to go with you before?" Lucy inquired.

"I did. One. Long time ago now."

"Yeah?" Lucy propped herself on her elbow so she could study his face, which was dusted with dark shadow. "What happened to her?"

"I don't know. She turned me down. I expect she's married with six kids by now."

Lucy stared at him in astonishment. "She turned you down? Was there something wrong with her?"

Again, the flash of smile. "I was a big, lumbering cowboy with not much to say. She figured she could do better."

Silly woman. Lucy rested her head on Hal's shoulder. "No, she couldn't." She let out a contented sigh. "I'd love to go steady with you, Hal."

"But ...?" He said it as though she'd voice a reservation.

"No buts." Lucy raised her head again. "Why should there be a but?"

Hal's shrug moved her body in a delicious way. "You had a bad breakup. You might not be over this Clyde guy. On the rebound."

Lucy sobered. "Clyde hurt me. He hurt me bad, I won't lie. I trusted him, and he threw that in my face. He didn't trust *me* enough to tell me what he planned to do. Didn't care about me enough. But it's been a year. I've had time to realize I really didn't lose anything."

"He's a dumbass," Hal said. "He didn't understand the treasure he had."

"You keep reminding me why I like you." Lucy traced his collarbone, his skin warm and still damp from their sweaty lovemaking. "I think I never knew the real Clyde. I superimposed my idea of the perfect guy onto him and didn't realize he didn't fit. I loved the image, not the reality. He ripped the blinders off the day he declared he was getting married to someone else. In that second, I saw everything in sharp clarity. He was an arrogant, selfish, self-centered asshole. I pity his wife now."

A growl rumbled Hal's chest. "I want to punch his face for what he did. So do your brothers."

"I know. It's so sweet you all want to. But please don't. He has lawyers who would put you in prison forever, and that's not the kind of relationship I want with you. Across a table, or through a glass with phones."

"Not really what I want either." Hal ran his broad fingers through her hair, sending warm sensations through her. "But that doesn't mean he should have done what he did without consequences. He was in the wrong, not you."

"I like you more and more." Lucy kissed his throat. "The

whole fiasco made me realize it was time to come home. To stop running away and figure out what I truly need from my life."

"Being ambitious isn't a bad thing," Hal pointed out. "To want a career, make some money, buy a nice house, maybe get a dog ..."

Lucy shook with laughter. "I hadn't taken it that far yet. But yeah, I was proud I'd learned to stand on my own feet and earn a living, without relying on my family. I saw myself working my way to the top of the stockbroking firm, and not just because I was the boss's son's girlfriend."

"You could have done it," Hal said. "You're smart enough."

If he kept up the compliments, Lucy was going to dissolve into warm goo. "What wasn't smart was getting involved with someone at work. I know now why people say to never do that. If it ends, it messes up both your personal life and your professional life. In my case, it got me fired."

"Why'd you decide to come straight back to Riverbend?" Hal asked, his tone curious and without judgment. "I bet any other company in Houston, or the state—hell, the whole country—would have snapped you up. You were good at your job, had experience, and like I said, smart. You could have worked for a rival company and taken his down."

"Yes, that would have been nice," Lucy agreed, gleefully imagining Clyde's despair when his dad's firm had to close its doors. His free ride would be over. "It crossed my mind. But I simply no longer had the energy. Plus, I didn't want the rest of my life driven by revenge on Clyde. I didn't want him to be that important. I was ready to get away from my job—from the trivial arguments, the fear I'd make the wrong decision at the wrong time and lose the company a shit-ton of money. The worry I'd not be invited to the right party or into the right meeting, and then my climb up the ladder would be even tougher. So much fear of missing out." She let out a breath. "And in the end, none of it *matters*."

"I don't know if it didn't matter," Hal said. "You did really well, didn't you?"

"I did. I was an asset to the company. But the minute I stepped out of line ..." Lucy snapped her fingers. "Everything I accomplished counted for nothing. I couldn't stay and start again. I wanted to come home, to a place where everything was easier."

Hal's chuckle vibrated Lucy in a pleasant way. "I don't know about easy. Small-town life can be complicated."

"It sure can be." Lucy squeezed her eyes shut then popped them open again. "I remembered that from day one. Trying to keep up my big smile so no one would know my life was one huge mess. Everyone either wanted to smother me in sympathy or crow that I should have known better than to try to leave Riverbend. I needed a job, so I didn't have to bunk in with Kyle and Anna—you do *not* want to be in the same house while they're getting busy under the covers. Then I realized I had feelings for you, and damn, was that confusing."

"You had feelings for me?" Hal gathered her closer. "I wish I'd known that. I had feelings for you, but I was pretty certain about them. It's not confusing for me at all."

A flood of contentedness penetrated the wall Lucy had built around herself. "I wasn't sure I could trust what I felt. I knew you were a terrific guy, and handsome, and seriously sexy, but I was afraid I was doing what you said—being on the rebound."

Hal's cheeks reddened. He wasn't as good at receiving compliments as giving them. "Is that why you backed off?"

Lucy blinked. "I backed off? When? You mean after we kissed at the B&B's opening?"

"Yep."

"*I* didn't back off. *You* backed off."

Hal frowned. "No, I didn't."

"You sure did. You didn't call, you didn't text. Then at Christmas, you came to Ray's when I invited you, but nothing happened."

"I wasn't sure what you wanted," Hal said in a reasonable tone. "If you were expecting me to tackle you and haul you into a closet, I couldn't do that. Not as a guest at Christmas dinner with a bunch of kids around."

Lucy bit back a laugh. "Well, I suppose not. We didn't get to talk much that day."

"Lots of people there."

True. At that party, as soon as she'd started across a room toward Hal, someone would intercept her and begin gabbing. She'd met Drew's friends from Chicago, with whom Lucy had a lot in common. Plus, Lucy's sister and brothers had been there with their spouses and children. Not really the environment for conducting a steamy romance.

"I'm trying to make it your fault," Lucy realized. "I've been too scared to embrace another relationship, so I decided you didn't want one with me."

Hal regarded her in astonishment. "Of course, I wanted one with you. But I was scared too. You'd been burned so bad —Kyle told me all about it, multiple times. I was trying to give you space."

"I have all the space I need, thank you." Lucy traced a curl on his chest. "You know, Hal, when a man is interested in a woman, he needs to tell her. We can be dense. Especially when wrapped up in our own world."

"Likewise."

Lucy kissed his smooth shoulder and then nuzzled his neck. "Maybe we could be wrapped up in our worlds together?"

Hal's lips in her hair gave her assurance. "Sounds like a good idea," he whispered.

Lucy raised her head to transfer her kiss to his mouth. Hal's returning kiss smoothed out all that had been tangled and snarled inside her for the past year.

She raised herself over him, fingers finding his very ready cock, and slid down onto him. Hal caught her, bringing her down to him, closing out the world to all but themselves.

———

"You understand why I have to talk to you, Hillman," Ross Campbell said later that evening as he walked into the shadowy darkness of Jack Hillman's motorcycle garage.

CHAPTER FOURTEEN

J ack laid down a wrench and buried his irritation at the interruption. He wasn't surprised the young sheriff had stepped so casually into Jack's garage. Ross, even when informal in civilian clothes, liked to be thorough.

Jack's small repair shop was attached to his building supply yard, and in it he fixed or enhanced motorcycles for residents and a few out-of-towners. He was fortunate that his reputation for decent work had spread, and he usually had enough business in this side operation to keep him happy.

"I'm trying to figure out what happened to Nate Redfern." Ross paused to admire a Softail Fat Boy that Jack had finished and polished, ready for its owner. "Someone was hurt in my jurisdiction, and I want to know who did it."

"I thought he was awake," Jack said. "I'd think a dickhead like that would shout accusations as soon as he opened his eyes."

"He swims in and out of consciousness," Ross answered. "His dad arrived to stay with him. I'd like to be able to tell him who nearly killed his son."

Jack lifted his hands, one holding a rag. "It wasn't me, officer. I have an alibi."

"You were with Karen," Ross stated. Sheriff Campbell didn't believe in being delicate, not when he was doing his job.

"I was."

"She corroborated," Ross said. "You're lucky, Hillman. Not many ladies would confess exactly what you were doing at the time in question."

Jack softened into a chuckle. "She's not shy, no. The question is—do you believe her?"

Ross folded his arms and leaned against the edge of a worktable. "I do, actually. She offered to give me details, but I asked her not to."

"She'd embellish." Jack couldn't stop his grin. Karen liked to talk up their private life as if they were having upside-down swinging-from-the-rafters very acrobatic sex.

That was a long way from reality. Jack and Karen—well, they weren't together. Not in the way Jack would like. Maybe Karen wanted to be, he didn't know. But Jack's life was complicated and getting more complicated by the minute.

Fortunately, he really had been with Karen Saturday night after he'd assisted the Campbells in shoving Redfern into a truck and sending him off. No rafter-swinging with Karen, but they'd been alone, and intimate.

"I didn't come to interrogate you about your love life," Ross said after another glance at the Harley. "Do you know of anyone capable of that level of assault? Someone who might have come into the area recently, I mean. I don't think whoever it was intended to kill Redfern. It was more like they were teaching him a lesson."

Jack adjusted the wrench he'd set on the tool bench. He liked his torque and socket wrenches lined up by size, so if he needed a certain one, he knew where to reach for it. His mentor had taught him that long ago.

"Why do you think they didn't mean to kill him?" he asked.

"The wounds were deliberate and delivered with precision," Ross answered. "It wasn't a random free-for-all fight. This person—or persons—could have killed him if they'd wanted to."

"That lets out Hal," Jack stated. "He's not a killer. Doesn't have the instinct."

"I realized that when I saw what had been done to Redfern. Hal would have punched him, but not the other things. I agree. Hal doesn't have the killer instinct." Ross eyed Jack evenly. "But you know people who do."

"Yep. Unfortunately."

"Any of them hanging around my county lately?"

Most days, Jack found Ross's territoriality about River County amusing. Ross's family had lived here for generations, so maybe it was natural that he kept his Campbell-blue eyes on everything.

Tonight, Jack felt as though he should be a little bit careful how he answered. "I'm not in touch with them anymore. But no, I haven't seen anyone I recognize."

"Mmm." Ross's noncommittal hum was unnerving. "How about anyone you *don't* recognize?"

"This is a small town," Jack pointed out. "You'd notice whoever I did."

"Yes, but from what Hal tells me, the guys from Nate's old crew would realize they needed to hide from me. But they might not bother hiding from you."

"Because I have a rep?" Jack considered this, not offended. "That's true. So far, though, I haven't seen anyone. I will keep my eyes peeled."

Ross unfolded himself, relaxing into a human being. "Thanks. I'd appreciate that." He gestured to the Harley without touching it. "Sweet ride."

"Yep." Jack looked over the bike with some pride. "Fixing it up for a friend." He let his eyes crinkle. "Not a criminal friend."

"If he ever wants to sell it ..." Ross left the offer hanging.

Jack thought about its owner and shook his head. "Doubt it. But I can keep a lookout for one like it."

"That would be great. Thanks for talking to me, Hillman."

"Always a pleasure, Campbell."

Ross's eyes twinkled. "Is it?"

"Hell, yes. You're a damn sight better than Hennessy ever was." The former sheriff had been corrupt as well as full of himself.

"I'll take that compliment and leave with it." Ross gave him a nod. "See you."

"Give my best to your mom," Hillman said. "And Sam."

Ross laughed. "I'll do that."

He took himself off then, climbing into his sheriff's SUV and pulling out into the road. The roar of his engine faded into the night.

The door to Jack's office opened, and Karen Marvin, sleek in a business suit, slipped out, patting her golden hair into place.

"Do you think he knew I was here?" she asked.

Karen, always neatly turned out in some kind of suit or slim dress, was incongruous in this garage with motorcycles in pieces, tools from small socket wrenches to large air compressors, and plenty of grease. Though Jack had learned to keep things fairly organized, a clean workshop meant that no one was actually working in it.

"Ross is pretty smart." Jack wiped off his hands and tossed the rag onto a table. "So, probably he did."

"I didn't want to embarrass you. Jack taking Karen for an after-dinner ride."

"Ross Campbell would never say that," Jack said. "His brothers would, but not Ross."

"That's true." Karen lifted a mirror that was ready to be installed on a bike and checked her face, doing the hair-pat thing again. "Well, I suppose it's time I got going."

"You don't have to." The words shot out of Jack's mouth before he could stop them.

Karen sent him one of her surprisingly warm smiles. "I have a bar to run. Another time."

"Sure thing."

It was always *another time*. They stole moments in Jack's office or hers, occasionally at her pristine home, but never at his place. They were like teenagers searching for a spot to hook up, Jack thought with exasperation. Never had time to savor the encounter, never had time to get to know each other.

Were either of them looking for something more permanent? Jack didn't know. Karen had been married several times and had famously declared she was finished with marriage. Jack's relationships in the past likewise had never ended well.

It was as if both of them knew they were heading for a collision and trying to find side roads to avoid it.

"I'd better get to work then," Karen said.

"Yeah. I'll see you later."

She lingered. "I could drive you home after."

She meant drive Jack to her place, where they'd steal more moments, have breakfast, and part ways.

Jack wouldn't mind—he'd decided to take what he could get and let this play out without forcing it.

"Can't," he said in true disappointment. "I have a client coming in early for his bike." He gestured to the Softail Ross had admired.

"So definitely another time, then."

Karen never fussed or ranted when they couldn't be together. She just agreed in her calm way to wait, and that was it.

"Sure," Jack repeated.

Karen set down the mirror and flashed him another smile. "Bye, then."

Jack intercepted her before she could open the door to the cool night. She gazed at him, startled, then softened when Jack cupped her cheek. He drew her up to him for a kiss—a deep, hot, tangling kiss only Karen could give.

When they parted, Karen rested her hand lightly on his chest. "I always look forward to seeing you, Jack."

"Likewise."

Karen hesitated, as if searching his eyes for something. Then she patted his chest with her slim fingers and slid out into the night. Soon he heard her car start with its usual purr.

Jack released a sigh as he shut the door. He hoped it wouldn't be too long and frustrating a time before he could taste her again.

———

Lucy woke in the morning in Hal's bed, with Hal snoozing next to her, feeling odd. She quietly regarded the ceiling and tried to pinpoint what this emotion was.

Then it struck her. She was happy.

It had been a very long time since she'd basked in contentedness, believing that life was good.

A seriously long time.

She lay still for a while, savoring the moment, fearing to
move and have it evaporate. Part of the reason for her state of
mind was the hunky bull rider sprawled next to her.

The other part was the fact that she'd finally let go. Lucy
had thought returning to Riverbend to lick her wounds would
not only be temporary but instantly heal her. She'd mourn for
a few weeks, then put Clyde and her life with him behind her
and stride out into the world, ready to be a corporate business-
woman once more.

After a year, she was still in Riverbend, and her ambitions
in the corporate direction had died. Not that she wanted to
hide for the rest of her life, abandoning any ideas of a career of
her own, but her desires to flee back to the wider world had
dissipated.

She liked her job as vet's assistant and accountant. She was
good at it, and she enjoyed working with the animals and with
Anna, who was a terrific human being as well as a great sister-
in-law. Lucy brought in enough money to pay the rent on her
house as well as for groceries, gas, clothes, and nights out with
her friends.

She'd reconnected with many of her childhood girlfriends
—the ones who'd stayed in Riverbend, anyway—and she'd
strengthened her bond with her sister and her two obnoxious
brothers. In addition, she now had adorable nieces and a
nephew to spoil. Her family was her anchor.

On top of that, Hal Jenkins lived in Riverbend. Hal the
handsome, strong, not-very-talkative cowboy who was always
there to lend a hand or a shoulder, and now a fabulous night
in bed.

Life couldn't get much better, could it? What Lucy had rediscovered in Riverbend was vastly superior to what she'd experienced outside it.

Hal snorted as he came awake, and rubbed a large hand over his face. He quickly turned his head, as though checking to make sure that Lucy was still there. His wide smile when he saw her made her hot all over.

It took them a while to get out of bed after that—the subsequent shower also took a lot of time.

"I'm going to be late." Lucy quickly buttoned her shirt afterward and tried to brush fingers through her damp hair. She'd learned to always carry a travel toothbrush in her purse in her business life, thank heavens. "Anna's a sweetheart, but she does expect me to be punctual. It's harder for her if I'm not."

Hal zipped himself into jeans and pulled a T-shirt over his broad chest. Lucy had to pause to watch and admire. "No worries. I'll drop you off on my way."

"The Kennedy ranch lies in an entirely different direction from the vet clinic," Lucy pointed out. "I'll call Anna and see if she can swing by here for me. Or Ray. He's closer."

Hal's big hands closed over Lucy's. "I am driving you," he said. "End of story."

His strength sent all kinds of fires dancing through her. "If you insist," Lucy said, not really fighting her surrender. "But then we'll both be late."

"Then we will. Breakfast?"

Hal briefly kissed her lips, stoking the heat, and released her. Lucy hurried after him as he strode from his bedroom toward the kitchen.

"You just said we'll be late."

"No reason to skip a good breakfast. It's the most important meal of the day."

Lucy burst out laughing. She braced herself on the kitchen doorframe and let herself be joyous. "Are you real?"

Hal pinched his arm, bared by his short sleeve. "I think so."

Lucy pushed herself from the doorframe and brushed past him to the refrigerator. "All right then. What are we going to fix?"

An hour later, after much laughter and banter, Lucy was full, energized, and ready to face the world. Hal turned out to be an amazing cook, serving eggs with cheese and salsa along with biscuits that were damn good. Lucy had brewed the coffee, which was more in line with her skillset.

As they rode toward town, the morning breeze coming through the open windows of Hal's truck, Lucy's ebullience began to ebb. Her night with Hal had been one of the best in her life. Would it ever happen again? Or would reality rush in to ruin everything, as usual?

Hal slowed to turn off the main highway, and soon afterward, they reached the vet's clinic. Only Anna's truck and her horseshoeing van sat in the lot—no patients yet, thank goodness.

Anna had opened the clinic's front door, likely on the lookout for Lucy. When she spied her in Hal's truck, she quickly disappeared back inside.

"So." Lucy rested her hand on the pickup's door handle, reluctant to open it, to step back into everyday life. She wanted to hold on to this bubble of happiness as long as she could.

"So." Hal didn't reach for her or lean to kiss her. "I guess we'll see each other Saturday night?"

"For our real date. I haven't forgotten."

"Good." Hal gripped the steering wheel like it was a lifeline. "I'm done at the rodeo at six. I'll shower and come pick you up."

That sounded official. Well, then. "Where are we going?"

"Don't know yet." Hal glanced from the door to the clinic to Lucy. "What would you like?"

Lucy, who was usually full of ideas when it came to going out, suddenly went blank. At this point, going anywhere with Hal was fine with her, as long as she could snuggle next to him and maybe wake up with him again. "Well, the diner's always close."

Hal blinked in amazement. "The diner? Not the fancy restaurant in White Fork?"

"Oh." For some reason Lucy hadn't pictured Hal putting on a suit to eat French food in a converted historic house. "Well, we could do that, I suppose."

Hal frowned at her hesitance. "I'll think of something."

"That's fine." This was getting awkward. Lucy opened the door. "See you Saturday night, then."

"Aren't you coming to the rodeo?" Hal asked.

"Oh. Yes. I am. Kyle is riding, and Anna will be there as the vet."

"Then I'll see you there."

Hal must think Lucy was a complete idiot. "Sure thing," she said brightly. "If I don't run into you before that. It's a small town."

Hal's scowl lightened as though he found her hilarious. "It is. You have a good day now."

Lucy thought she just might. "You, too."

Instead of waiting for Hal to make a move, Lucy leaned over and pulled him into a kiss.

The kiss turned interesting, full of promise. Hal brushed a knuckle over her cheek when they drew apart, which made

Lucy want to forget about her job, throw caution to the wind, and urge him to drive somewhere, anywhere. To hell with real life.

But Lucy had learned long ago to be sensible. She needed her job and Hal needed his. Other people relied on them.

She lightly swept her fingertips over his lips and forced herself to leave the truck. Watching Hal drive away was one of the hardest things Lucy had ever done.

Anna opened the door the instant Lucy hurried to the clinic's entrance.

"I was about to call you," Anna said. "But now I understand. I'm going to guess Hal didn't find you hitchhiking on the side of the road?"

"You can guess all you want to." Lucy's euphoria from her night with Hal returned, kicking aside any doldrums that tried to form. "I don't mind at all."

Anna laughed knowingly and led the way into the office.

———

HAL GRABBED HIS PHONE WITH RELIEF WHEN IT PEALED. He didn't think it would be Lucy, but he'd been wandering the ranch in a daze since he'd arrived, unable to keep his mind on his work. Hell, he was lucky he'd made it in one piece after dropping Lucy at the vet's without driving into a ditch or something.

His thoughts returned constantly to Lucy—to her laughter, her kisses, the way her face softened when he slid into her. She'd made love with everything she had, no holding back, her openness pouring all kinds of joy through him.

Pure, sharp desire was new to him. Of course, he'd had sex before and enjoyed it, but this had been intense beyond words.

All Hal could think about was being inside Lucy's sweet body and hope that he could be there again.

"Hello," he almost sang into the phone without bothering to notice the caller ID. "This is Jenkins. Who's this?"

"Ross Campbell. You're in a good mood."

"Well, it's a nice day, isn't it?"

"It is," Ross answered with amusement, as though he suspected Hal was happy about more than the weather. "I hope I don't ruin it with what I'm about to tell you."

"What?" Hal tried to focus and be serious, but it wasn't easy.

"Redfern has been moved out of intensive care. He's asking to see you. Can you get yourself to the medical center? As in right now?"

CHAPTER FIFTEEN

E ven having to request a few hours off from Mr. Kennedy, after he'd been late, and making the long drive to the medical center that lay between Riverbend and White Fork didn't dampen Hal's spirits. Lucy was the most amazing woman he'd ever met, and she acted as though she wanted to be with him.

The fact that she'd expected him to take her to the diner on their date had thrown him a little, but she probably hadn't thought an oxen-like cowboy would be interested in fancy restaurants. Fancy or not fancy—it didn't matter to Hal. Good food was good food, no matter what restaurant was wrapped around it.

He'd give it some thought, though, and try to come up with a solution before Saturday night.

The medical center was fairly quiet when he entered. Ross, in uniform, waited in the main floor lobby. The only other occupant besides the staff was a woman clutching the hand of a little girl, speaking worriedly to the nurse at the reception desk.

Ross gave both mother and daughter—the girl regarded Ross in awe—a sympathetic nod and led Hal into an elevator.

"Redfern's dad's with him," Ross said quietly. "Redfern started asking for you early this morning, but I decided I'd give you a few hours."

Hal flushed, remembering what he'd been doing early this morning. "I appreciate that."

Ross shot him a look as though he knew damn well that Lucy had been with him but chose to say nothing. "His dad came in last night. I was surprised he waited so long, but he claims he only got word yesterday morning."

"Surprised he's here at all," Hal said. "Kent Redfern is a mean son-of-a-bitch. Not a lot of warm fatherliness in him that I've ever seen. But who knows? I suppose when your kid is hurt, you come."

"Not all parents do," Ross said. "The bad part of my job is seeing people at their worst."

The elevator doors opened at that point, cutting off conversation. Redfern had been put on the top floor where the badly injured went to heal once they were out of intensive care.

Nate had apparently been given a private room at the end of the ward. Thin carpeting muffled Hal's and Ross's footsteps as they traversed the hall beyond the nurse's station.

They passed a bull rider Hal recognized, who limped by in his back-opening hospital gown, dragging a metal stand draped with bags of clear liquid. He gave Hal a nod, as though they were passing in the bar.

"Jenkins."

"Buchanan. Hope you're doing better."

The man had been injured during a practice run for this Saturday. It was safe to say he'd not be in the competition.

"Better than I was," Buchanan said. "You visiting Redfern?"

Hal acknowledged this with a brief nod.

Buchanan sent Ross a sideways glance and then muttered, "Dopers suck."

"They do," Hal agreed. He and Ross went on by, both studiously not noticing how Buchanan's gown exposed his very bare ass.

Nate's room was full of beeping machines. IV drips like the ones Buchanan had been toting snaked into Nate's arm, and a whiteboard with notes about Nate's condition hung on the wall. Not great, was their gist.

Nate's bandaged arm rested in a sling across his chest and a device held his jaw in place. Unable to turn his head, Nate swiveled his eyes to the door when he saw Hal, and a flush darkened his bruised and abraded face.

Another man barreled into the room after Hal and Ross, as though sure they were there to mess with the vulnerable Nate. He was about a head shorter than Hal, and lean and ropy. He had iron gray hair but otherwise greatly resembled the younger man flat on his back in the bed.

Kent Redfern, Nate's father.

"Hal Jenkins," Kent said. It was less a greeting than a statement.

Hal gave him a nod. "Redfern." He glanced at Nate who glared from behind his tubes and wires. "How is he?"

"He'll live." Another statement without inflection. "No thanks to you."

"I didn't do this to him," Hal said.

Kent's expression said he knew it was futile to argue. "I'm here to see what this joke of a hospital can do for Nate, then

I'm taking him home, where he'll be safe. What are *you* doing?"

From the limited facial movement Nate could make, Hal saw he didn't relish the idea of being under his dad's care. Hal didn't blame him. Kent had let Nate be tried and imprisoned for doping charges, while he'd presented all kinds of proof that he himself hadn't been involved. Kent hadn't labored very hard to protect Nate and had told the press that he'd always been disappointed in his son.

"Nate said he wanted to speak to me," Hal replied.

"Huh. He can't talk." Kent sneered. "Never says much worth hearing on his best days."

Nate closed his eyes. Kent folded his arms, unwilling to move, but Hal guessed Nate wouldn't say a word with his father next to him. He sent Ross a glance.

Ross understood. "Mr. Redfern," he said in his official sheriff tones. "Will you step into the hall with me?"

Kent jerked his gaze to Ross. "What for?"

"A few questions I need to ask you." Ross waited in seeming patience but also with the bearing that wouldn't take no for an answer.

"I'm not leaving my son alone with the man who put him in this stupid hospital."

"Hal had nothing to do with it," Ross said easily. "I assure you." He gestured for Kent to precede him out.

Kent scowled but finally huffed and strode from the room. Ross followed, pulling the door closed behind him.

Hal lingered in the empty space between door and bed, uncertain of what to say to Nate. The man becoming a victim didn't mean he'd be any less a villain when he recovered, but pity stirred Hal's compassion.

Nate's face was dark with bruises. Abrasions lay under

both eyes and around his mouth. He had broken ribs as well as a broken arm, plus some internal bleeding that had required surgery, so the whiteboard indicated. His road to recovery would be long.

"Do you know who did this to you?" Hal asked.

Fierce rage shone in Nate's eyes, and he gave Hal the barest hint of a nod.

"You can tell me," Hal went on, as he slowly approached the bed. "Ross is good at what he does. He'll make sure they pay *and* leave you alone. No retaliation."

Nate's skepticism was evident. He couldn't shake his head no, but he closed his eyes as though resigned.

Hal had to admit he wasn't certain whether the assailants would leave Nate alone or not. Nate had pissed off a lot of people, and drug peddlers tended to have long memories.

"How about you just tell *me*." Hal halted at the bed, gazing down at Nate with what he hoped was a reassuring expression. "I can take care of them. Me and some friends."

He'd drag the perpetrators to Ross after he, Jack, the Campbells, and the Mallorys had put the fear of God into them, but Nate didn't need to know that.

Nate's free arm moved slightly, and he twitched his fingers as though beckoning Hal closer. Hal bent down, hoping Nate would whisper the names of the culprits.

Nate's voice was raw, low, and barely discernable as he forced out the words through his teeth. "Don't. Go." He paused and drew a breath for strength before continuing. "To. Rodeo." He sank back into his pillow, spent.

"Don't go to the rodeo?" Hal repeated in a quiet voice. "You mean the one this Saturday?" Nate gave him another barely perceptible nod. "Why not?"

He got a scowl for an answer. Nate was exhausted, Hal could see, and had said all he could.

Were Nate's words a warning or a threat? What would happen at the rodeo that Nate didn't want Hal to encounter?

Hal gave Nate's good shoulder a gentle pat. "I'll consider what you said. And Ross will get these guys, I swear to you. He's good—his whole department is."

Nate managed to convey disbelief and disgust at Hal's faith in the law. He closed his eyes again, sucking in another long breath.

Hal turned to go. Before he reached the door, he heard Nate say, "Help. Me."

Hal swung back, but Nate's eyes were sealed shut, his body relaxing as he slid into medicated slumber.

Hal regarded him for some time before he opened the door to join Ross and Nate's father in the hall.

Kent immediately pushed past Hal and marched into the room, ignoring Hal and Ross as the door swung shut behind him.

"Did he tell you who did this?" Ross asked, keeping his voice down.

Hal shook his head. "I don't know why he won't, but probably he fears he'll get worse if he names the culprits." He paused a beat. "I think something might happen at the rodeo this weekend. Nate mentioned that. Told me not to go."

Ross's dark brows went up. "Interesting. Does he expect the dopers to strike again?"

"Possibly. Or something will go down that he doesn't want me to see."

Ross studied the closed door thoughtfully. "Okay. Extra security at the rodeo. We'll stop them, whoever they are. Would you recognize Nate's old colleagues?"

"Sure," Hal said. "I worked around them long enough."

"Then please keep your eye out for them at the rodeo this weekend and report anything to me or my deputies."

Ross Campbell was young, a new father, and considered the runt of the Campbell litter. He'd not followed in his brothers' bootsteps to become stunt riders and horse trainers but had beaten his own path.

Yet, Ross knew how to command. He never had to raise his voice—he only looked at a person with his stern blue eyes, and that person found himself nodding obediently, as Hal did now.

"I'll do that."

"Good." Ross lost his sheriff's demeanor. "Say hi to Lucy for me."

"Will do."

Hal pretended he felt no embarrassment that the world guessed that he and Lucy had been together last night. Then again, why should he be embarrassed? Lucy was a beautiful woman, and the sooner Hal saw her again, the better.

He and Ross exchanged farewells, Ross staying to see if he could get more out of Kent or Nate.

Hal lifted a hand to the nurses at their station and Buchanan on his next round through the hallway, then he departed the clinic. Thoughts of Lucy filled his head and his heart, making the bleak surroundings of the medical center take on a rosy glow.

———

MANNY JUDD HAD ASSUMED THAT ONCE HE'D FINALLY graduated high school, he'd immediately become a wise and experienced adult.

He still felt like a stupid kid in many ways, even though he had a great job helping manage the stables at Callie Jones-Campbell's horse rehab ranch. Plus, he was going out with Tracy Harrison, who'd also recently graduated and now attended River County's community college.

Tracy was way more sophisticated than he was, Manny mused as he contemplated Tracy in the front seat of his pickup. Her brother was one of Ross Campbell's deputies, which made other guys afraid of going near her.

Manny was wary of Deputy Harrison himself, though Joe had proved to be a pretty nice guy, and fine with Manny dating his little sister. Okay, mostly fine with Manny dating his sister.

Tracy herself was wonderful. With her beautiful brown eyes and heart-melting smile, Manny was on his way to being madly in love. He figured Tracy would realize any second that Manny was a loser and find a real guy to go out with, but in the meantime, Manny was going to enjoy the hell out of their relationship.

Tonight, they'd decided to drive to an outdoor music festival being held on the highway to Johnson City. A band he and Tracy both liked was playing. Why not?

The venue lay about ten miles south of Riverbend. By the time Manny and Tracy arrived, the parking lot was full of cars, trucks, and motorcycles, with the stage lit up and ready.

The lavishly tattooed young woman who took their tickets gave them a purple band for their wrists that proclaimed they weren't yet of legal drinking age. Close, though, Manny thought. In a couple years, he and Tracy could party hard—if Tracy still liked him by then.

Manny kept a tight hold of Tracy's hand as he squeezed through men and women who were milling around, drinking, laughing, and shouting to each other as they waited for the show to start. Recorded music pumped from speakers at a high volume, priming the crowd for the first group.

Manny steered Tracy to the table where they could buy non-alcoholic beverages, and procured her a can of soda, getting one for himself. They sipped, exchanged greetings with people they knew from town, and enjoyed the sensation of being out on their own without brothers, parents, or Sheriff Campbell breathing down their necks.

When the band came on, Manny and Tracy surged forward excitedly with the crowd. The group came from Dallas, had a kick-ass woman guitarist, and played grungy Texas blues. They were awesome.

A man slammed past Manny to get closer to the stage. He was big and crashed into Manny at the correct angle to splash sticky soda all over Manny's shirt. The man's three friends burst out laughing, and the first guy turned back.

"Sorry, kid."

"Hey, it's no problem." Manny held onto his temper and kept his tone neutral. The man didn't offer to replace his drink, as Manny had known he wouldn't.

Once they were gone, Manny quietly grasped Tracy's elbow and led her to the edge of the crowd.

"What's the matter?" Tracy yelled into his ear over the screeching guitar. "Do you know those guys?"

"Yep." Manny tried to keep his voice from shaking. "I used to sort-of know them. They're bad news."

Tracy stared at him in concern. "Didn't look like they recognized you."

"I stayed on the fringes of their crowd," Manny said into her ear. He didn't mind having to put his lips close to her or have her soft hair tickling his nose. "I was ten. An errand boy."

"You think they came to cause trouble?"

The four burly cowboys Manny remembered from his misspent youth had reached the stage and were raising beers, yelling their appreciation. The guitarist in a tank top, tatts down her arms, ignored them while she shredded her guitar, all her attention for her music.

"Nah, I think they're just here for the band." Manny's instincts, honed from keeping himself alive, were shouting at him. "But they're bad people. They hire themselves sometimes to worse ones."

Tracy's brow furrowed with worry. "Should I tell my brother?"

Manny shrugged. "They're not doing anything." Yet.

"Okay." Tracy took his hand and squeezed it. "I love this song. Let's not let them ruin it."

"Right." Manny shut up so they could listen to the rest of it. The guitarist was going nuts on her guitar while the singer, a deep-voiced dude, belted out the tune.

Everyone screamed when it was done, including the bullies from Manny's bad old days.

Another song began, the musicians sweating in the warm spring air. Manny loved this one too, but he couldn't shake the uneasy feeling, which made his scalp prickle.

"Let's get out of here," he said to Tracy.

"Are you sure? They've barely started."

"I'm sure. Sorry. I'll make it up to you."

Tracy followed his gaze to the goons in front of the stage. She was smarter than any other girl Manny had ever known, and she didn't question his concerns.

"Okay," Tracy said. "They played my favorite song first, and we'll catch them another time."

Manny relaxed in relief that she understood. Hand-in-hand, they threaded their way out to the relative quiet of the parking lot.

"You're spooked," Tracy said. "I think I *will* tell my brother."

"Yeah." Manny shrugged but didn't let go of Tracy's hand. "Maybe it's just bad memories. But I thought they'd left River County for good. Why'd they come back? Wasn't just to watch the band, I'll bet."

"I'll give Joe a call when we get back to town," Tracy said. "Want to go to the diner?"

"Sure." Manny abandoned all pretense at being grown up. "Mrs. Ward's got her fresh cherry pies ready now."

"Mmm." Tracy hummed in agreement. "I love cherry pie. With lots of whipped cream."

"Oooh, let's get us some of that." Manny led Tracy to the truck at a run, both of them laughing.

Manny opened the door for Tracy then sprinted for the driver's seat, landing in it, out of breath. Tracy grinned at him and reached for his hand again, and Manny's heart turned over.

How the hell did he get so lucky?

Manny started up the truck and spun out of the lot, needing to put plenty of space between himself and the men who'd terrified him as a kid, the ones who could not be up to any good.

CHAPTER SIXTEEN

The first appointment Wednesday morning for Anna and Lucy was at Callie's rehab ranch. She and Anna routinely paid a call on the old Morgan place where Callie and her business partner rehabilitated horses that had been abandoned, abused, or needed a little extra TLC after a surgery or illness. Dr. Anna was the official vet for the ranch, and she and Lucy drove out to look over the animals each week and treat those that needed it.

This morning was lovely, blue skies and cool breezes, both the cold of winter and the coming heat of summer at bay for now.

Once she'd parked the truck, Anna scuttled into the whitewashed barn, her hand on her back, which had been aching. However, she refused to let aches and pains stop her from checking up on the horses, she'd declared when Lucy suggested they skip the visit today.

Lucy had known Anna wouldn't listen. She was dedicated —some might say stubborn. Lucy and Callie watched in resignation as Anna waddled into the line of stalls, giving helloes to the horses she passed like they were old friends.

Manny Judd, former juvenile delinquent and now reformed stable manager at Callie's ranch, had greeted Anna with his usual sunny enthusiasm. Now, smile gone, he turned to Callie, and in tones that he probably meant to be discreet demanded, "Are you going to tell her?"

Callie, the beautiful former debutante, was adorable in her jeans and boots, flannel shirt with rolled up sleeves. She peered uneasily at Lucy, leaving no doubt as to who was the "her" in that sentence.

"Tell me what?" Lucy asked.

Callie shot Manny an unhappy gaze. "Lucy has enough to worry about."

"No, I don't," Lucy stated. "What is it, Manny?"

In spite of Callie's scowl, Manny plunged ahead. "Saw some guys at the festival grounds last night. Tracy told Deputy Harrison about them, and Deputy Harrison told Sheriff Ross. Callie says Ross thinks they might have been the ones who beat up Nate Redfern."

"Oh yeah?" Lucy's spirits lifted. "Good. Ross can go arrest them and leave Hal in the clear." She glanced between Callie and Manny, realizing that neither of them seemed happy. "Is there more? What's the matter?"

"If they did the beating, they didn't come up with the idea on their own," Manny said. "They're bad guys, but they usually work for worse guys."

"Oh." The implications of Manny's information stirred worry. "You think someone from Nate's old crew called in a hit." They wouldn't have to leave prison to hire bone-breakers.

"Yep," Manny confirmed. "And if these dopers are taking

their revenge or whatever, on people in their past, Ross thinks Hal might be next."

"Does he?" Lucy said in alarm. "Did Ross warn Hal?"

"He did," Callie answered. "Hal of course refuses to stay home and lock the doors, but Ross sent Rafe to keep an eye on him."

Rafe Sanchez was another of the deputies, very competent, and friends with Hal.

Not that Hal had reported any of this to Lucy. Knowing Hal, he'd probably been trying to keep her safe and handle it on his own.

"Damn it." Lucy reached for her phone. "Thank you for telling me, Manny."

She scrolled to Hal's number, but she hesitated, thumb hovering. What would she say to him? Scold him for going to work as usual? Tell him to do what Sanchez told him? Admonish him for not keeping her in the loop?

Did they have the kind of relationship where Hal should keep her in the loop? Lucy had no idea now that she thought about it. They'd slept together—which had been wonderful—and they were friends, but did things go deeper?

The burning in her heart told Lucy she wanted them to be deeper. Needed them to be.

Just as her thumb connected with the phone, Anna yelled from somewhere inside the barn.

Lucy cancelled the call as soon as the screen showed the number ringing and dashed with Callie and Manny along the line of stalls. She pictured all kinds of dire situations—Anna on the ground with a horse trampling her, or one with its teeth firmly in her neck, lifting the small woman up to shake her. Or Anna flat on her back after one had kicked the hell out of her. Sweet God, she could lose the baby.

Lucy stumbled to a halt, Callie and Manny nearly running into her, when she found Anna at the other end of the open barn, seated on an overturned crate, her arms around her belly. Anna rocked back and forth, moaning. Horses, safely in their stalls and nowhere near her, watched over the stall doors, ears pricked, eyes fixed on Anna.

Lucy crouched on one knee next to her. "Anna? You all right?"

Anna lifted her head, fear, annoyance, and excitement warring in her eyes. "I'm nine months pregnant and having contractions. My diagnosis—this baby is coming."

"Wow." Lucy's heartbeat raced, hysterical joy bubbling inside her. "That's terrific. Let's get you up."

Manny whooped and punched the air, causing horses to dance back in alarm. "Baby!" he yelled. "Baby, baby. Let's go!"

Callie, the calmest of them all, came to Anna's other side and joined Lucy in assisting her to her feet. "It will be fine," Callie assured her. "Dr. Sue is brilliant. She did great with me and Caleb. Not to mention every other child in this town. Can you walk?"

Anna spoke through clenched teeth. "I'll have to, won't I?"

"Nah," Manny said. "We have that gurney we use for the horses. Want me to grab it?"

Anna glared at him. "No!"

"Are you sure? I bet it would work."

Manny's cheerful suggestion motivated Anna to hobble out of the barn, supported by Lucy and Callie. They got Anna to her truck, Manny loping alongside and informing Anna that horses popped out babies all the time with no trouble.

Lucy and Callie tucked Anna into her passenger seat, and Lucy took the keys from her.

Lucy's hands were shaking, excitement gripping her more

than she'd anticipated it would. But Anna and Kyle were having a baby. She'd be an aunt. Okay, she was already an aunt, but every time it was terrific.

"Kyle," Anna gasped. She pulled her phone from her jacket pocket but clenched it hard when another contraction hit her.

"Want me to call him?" Callie asked as Lucy made for the driver's seat.

"No, let me," Lucy sang. She climbed into the truck and started it. "Please. I want to be the one who makes my brother pass out."

Callie laughed, and Manny did another whoop. "Tell me *everything*," Callie commanded, and Lucy pulled away.

"Be nice to him," Anna said as Lucy stopped at the entrance to the ranch and popped up Kyle's number on her own phone. Her call to Hal had vanished, disappearing into the ether.

"I'll try," Lucy said.

"Put it on speaker. I want to hear this."

Anna's truck was too old to allow Lucy to plug in and broadcast the call through the vehicle's system, but she held up the phone as it rang.

"Yeah?" Kyle's drawl came through. "Lucy? What's up?"

"Your wife's having a baby," Lucy chirped. "Right this minute. We're on the way to the clinic. You want to come?"

Both she and Anna burst out laughing at the dead silence that greeted the question, stated oh-so-casually.

"Kyle?" Anna inquired as the silence went on. "You all right?"

There was a crackling noise, and then Hal Jenkins's voice replied, "I'll get him there," he announced. "Kyle's got his head between his knees right now. We're at Fuller's Hardware. I'll pry him up and drive him over."

"Thanks, Hal." Lucy gazed longingly at the phone as though she could see Hal's handsome face through its dark screen.

"Did you try to call me before?" Hal asked. "Looking for Kyle?"

"No." Lucy revved the engine, flustered. "I mean yes. But no. I mean—I'll talk to you later. We gotta go."

She thumbed the phone off and tossed it into the cubby under the dash, then peeled out of the ranch's drive. Beside her, Anna groaned with another contraction, and Lucy reached for her hand.

"You hang tight, Anna. I'll get you there."

Lucy let out a whoop worthy of Manny and spun the truck onto the road, laughing in exhilaration.

———

HAL ENTERED THE CLINIC JUST AS LUCY ACCOMPANIED Anna, wheeled in a chair by an orderly, to the elevators. Kyle had already burst in ahead of Hal, barely waiting for the sliding doors to open before he charged through.

"Hey, baby," Kyle panted as he slid to a halt in front of Anna. "I'm here. I'm here."

Anna clasped Kyle's hands and smiled up at him, her radiant love for him apparent.

"You look green," Lucy said to Kyle. "Maybe they should defib you."

Kyle ignored his sister's banter. "Thanks for bringing her," he said to Lucy.

The elevator doors opened. The orderly pushed Anna in, Kyle right next to her.

"I wasn't about to let her drive." Lucy winked at Kyle. "You two enjoy some alone time. I'll be up to visit later."

Kyle turned all his attention to his wife, and the doors closed, shutting out the scene.

Hal swallowed the lump in his throat and then found himself facing Lucy, whose cheeriness had gone.

"Can I talk to you, Hal?" she asked. "Someplace a little less public?"

The clinic's lobby was fairly deserted, but Hal gave her a nod. Lucy led the way to the cafeteria, her mouth tight, which did not stop Hal admiring her graceful stride.

They ordered coffees, which Hal paid for before Lucy could, and found a small table in a corner. Windows lined this room, and their table was bathed in sunshine on two sides.

"What's up?" Hal prayed that the next words out of Lucy's mouth wouldn't be, *This isn't going to work.* Or, *I need some space.* Or, worst of all, *It's not you, it's me.*

"Why didn't you tell me Ross thinks you're in danger?" Lucy demanded. "I heard about the goons Manny spied last night. Manny thinks they're thugs for hire, and Ross says whoever hired them will come after you next."

"Whoa, whoa. Slow down." Hal held up his hands. "There's nothing to say they'll definitely come after me."

Lucy's glare could have boiled the already cooling coffee. "There's nothing to say they *won't*. There are bad people out there, and you pissed them off by sending them to prison."

"I know. And I'm being careful, I promise. But I don't want you to worry about all this."

Her look changed to one of amazement. "Why shouldn't I worry about it?"

"Because this is my problem. I'll take care of things. I won't let you be hurt because of it."

Lucy's fury made Hal realize he'd said the wrong thing yet again. He wished he understood how to talk to women.

"I am not upset about this because I'm afraid I'll be hurt," Lucy informed him. "I'm afraid *you'll* be hurt. Then it will be *me* visiting *you* upstairs because your ribs are broken, and your jaw is wired shut." Lucy paused to draw a shaking breath. "What did Nate say to you yesterday, when you saw him? Is he going to be okay?"

Hal had texted Lucy that Ross had taken him to see Nate, but not the details. He thought about Nate's warning that he shouldn't go to the rodeo on Saturday. As much as he didn't want to convey this to Lucy, he also didn't want to lie to her.

"He asked me to help him."

Lucy's anger at Hal lessened the slightest bit. "Help him do what?"

"I don't know. He's scared. I don't like to think about what scares a bully like Redfern."

"Very bad people." Lucy tapped the table to emphasize her words. "Bad people who might be targeting you next."

"He also said I shouldn't go to the rodeo," Hal said slowly. "He didn't say why, specifically."

"There." Lucy opened her hands, palm up. "See? He's right—you shouldn't go."

"I still don't know if he meant I was in danger, or that something will go down there that he doesn't want me to stop." Hal closed his fingers around his cup to prevent himself from reaching for Lucy. "I can't really trust him, even when he's banged up. Redfern's not known for his integrity."

"Even so, tell Ross, and stay home."

Hal set his coffee back on the table with a thump. "I did tell Ross, and staying home is not gonna happen."

"Why not? Don't you want to remain in one piece? I think you shouldn't have even gone to work today." Lucy softened her tone. "Although it was lucky you were on hand to drive Kyle."

"Sure was. I stopped in at Fuller's for some supplies, and Kyle was there doing the same. That's when you called him." Hal let mirth trickle through his worry. "He wasn't in any shape to drive, so I offered him a ride."

"Same with me and Anna." Lucy's eyes shone with happiness for Anna and her brother, then they clouded over again. "Even so, stay home and lock your doors until Ross and the deputies say it's all clear."

Hal rested his arms on the table. "I appreciate your concern, Luce, but I learned a long time ago that I can't let bullies run my life. They're dangerous, yeah, but instead of hiding from them, I'm going make sure they stop. I came to Riverbend to get away from that life, but it didn't help, did it?"

"You appreciate my concern?" Lucy repeated his words with indignation. "I'm trying to say I don't want you hurt— ever. And *you're* going to stop these guys? How? And why? Ross knows what he's doing. Let him do it."

"I don't mean by myself. I mean helping Ross however I can. So will Jack, and the Campbells, and your brothers."

Lucy's eyes widened when Hal said the last. "Right, get my brothers beat up as well. Kyle's upstairs becoming a dad, for Pete's sake."

"Lucy, tell me what you want me to say." Hal abandoned his reticence and looked her square in the eyes. "I'm not going to run from this crew for the rest of my life. We're going to stop them before anyone else gets hurt. Including you."

"I'll be fine." Lucy stabbed her forefinger to her chest. "I'm not the one chasing bad guys all over the county."

Hal caught her hand. "No, but you'll be a target as much as I am. These are the kind of people who would hurt you to make me behave, like Redfern would have. Everyone knows how much I care about you."

Lucy stilled, eyes flickering as though she hadn't heard him correctly. "How much you ... care about me?"

"Hell, yes." Hal saw no reason to hide it. "I care a lot. Have for a while now."

"Everyone knows this, you say?"

He shrugged. "Pretty much. I thought you knew it too."

"No." Lucy gazed at him, stunned. "You don't actually say much, Hal."

"Never can find the right words. But yeah, you're special to me." Hal squeezed her hands. "Couldn't do what we did night before last if I didn't feel that way."

"Well, you're special to me." Lucy's voice went soft. "That's why I want you to hide in your basement until this goes away."

"Don't have a basement," Hal pointed out. "My house is on a concrete slab. Been thinking about moving, though. To something bigger."

"Really? Where would you—?" Lucy withdrew her hands to wave both in exasperation. "Don't distract me with house shopping. I want you to stay safe. I don't want anything to happen to you. That would kill me, I think."

Hal's heart squeezed. He wondered if Lucy exaggerated, but what was in her eyes told Hal that he'd somehow been lucky enough for this beautiful woman to be this anxious for him.

He had no idea how to go forward. Hal knew he had to

resolve the problems from his past or neither he nor Lucy could ever live in security. No contentment, always looking over their shoulders.

Hal needed to talk to Nate again, alone, without his dad hovering.

He gently grasped Lucy's hands once more. "It would kill me if something happened to *you*. Leave a hole in my life so big, I don't know what would fill it again."

Lucy gazed at him in bewilderment, her eyes moist. "I don't want a hole in my life either."

Hal slid back until only their fingertips touched. "Let me fix this, and then we can talk."

"Fix it how?" Lucy blinked away tears. "I'm scared for you, Hal. Wait, I know—we'll book a flight and go to Tahiti." She brightened. "Hey, that sounds like a great idea."

"Little problem of having to work," Hal reminded her.

"True." Lucy deflated. "Now that Anna will be out, I'll be seriously busy helping the interim vet settle in."

"And I'm committed to rodeos, not to mention integrating Kennedy's new cattle into the herds."

"I guess we're just working stiffs." Lucy's smile warmed even this barren cafeteria. "Doesn't mean we can't plan a vacation. I hear Tahiti is very nice."

"I'll leave that up to you," Hal said. "But I'm not wearing a speedo."

Lucy's laughter eased the last of his tension. He abruptly knew what he must do—everything in stark clarity. It was time to act.

Hal squeezed Lucy's hands once more and released them. "I'm going upstairs to talk to Nate."

Lucy immediately shoved back her chair. "I'm coming with you."

"Best you don't."

Hal wasn't sure why he'd expected her to listen. "He might tell me something he wouldn't tell you," she pointed out. "You distract his dad, and I'll get Nate to explain everything."

Hal wasn't about to agree to this scenario, but he ceased arguing. Lucy would simply follow him if he ordered her to stay behind. She wasn't the sort who meekly obeyed commands.

"Come on, then," Hal said in resignation.

They disposed of their coffee cups and left the mostly empty cafeteria to take the elevator to the top floor. Ross had asked the White Fork police to station a uniformed officer near Nate's room, but Hal didn't see one anywhere as they emerged from the elevator and approached the nurse's station.

"Hey, Lucy." The nurse on duty at the desk, whose name tag read *Lily*, was about Lucy's age. Her short black hair was combed neatly, her scrubs uncreased. "Hey, Hal."

"Lily," Hal greeted her. "Here to see Nate Redfern."

The young woman shook her head. "He's gone. His dad checked him out this morning."

Hal halted, alarm surging. "Where did he take him?"

"Home, I imagine. Let me check." Lily peered intently at her computer screen, fingers rapidly clicking a mouse. "Doctors wanted him to stay but his dad kicked up a fuss. Said Nate wasn't safe here." She frowned at the screen. "It doesn't say where they went. Only address we have is one in San Angelo."

"No way Nate was up to a drive to San Angelo," Hal stated. The city was about a hundred and eighty miles from Riverbend, which would be several hours in a car. With Nate's injuries, though, Hal would be surprised if the man could make it through the parking lot.

"That's all I know," Lily said regretfully. "Sorry."

Hal tapped the desk. "That's all right. Thank you."

He turned away. Lucy said her farewells to Lily and followed Hal to the elevators.

"Maybe it's for the best," Lucy suggested. "You said his dad was tough. He probably believes he can protect his son better than a police guard at a hospital. If Nate's dad has the right kind of friends, that could be true."

"Could be."

What Lucy said was logical, but Hal had a bad feeling he couldn't shake. Kent Redfern was not a man to be messed with, but there had to be something more going on. Hal would have to put out his own feelers to discover what had happened to Nate and his father.

He was reaching for the down button when Lily called to them, her voice rising in delight.

"Oh, hey, Lucy? I just heard from maternity. Message for you. Dr. Anna is having that baby right now!"

CHAPTER SEVENTEEN

Lucy's uneasiness about Nate and his absence departed on wings of giddiness. She slammed the elevator call button with two fingers and danced on her toes in impatience as the slow lift churned its way to the top floor.

When the elevator finally arrived, Hal's hand on Lucy's back steadied her as she zoomed inside. She suddenly couldn't remember what floor they needed to go to, but Hal reached around her to press the number two.

Lucy thanked him, her spirits high. Hal was right beside her, his touch still on her back, and he'd tacitly agreed to go to Tahiti with her. No matter what it took, Lucy was going to make it happen.

Warm sun, beaches, fruity drinks, and Hal next to her wearing very little. He was wrong. He had the body to rock a speedo.

When the elevator doors opened, the first person Lucy saw was her sister, Grace.

"I made them search the hospital for you," Grace said as Lucy impulsively hugged her. "Phone signals don't work well in here. I sent about twenty texts before I remembered that. Oh, hey, Hal."

"Grace." Hal gave her a nod, polite as ever. "How's Kyle holding up?"

"He's about to shit his pants," Grace said in delight. "Mom and Miles are on their way. Same with Ray and Drew. They're picking up Faith. Carter has Zach—Carter's the only one calm about this."

"Not every day your brother and his sweet wife have their first baby," Lucy agreed. "Of course, I remember what Jess told me about the day you had Zach. Carter was *not* calm then."

"No." Grace laughed.

Lucy hugged Grace again. If she'd hesitated over her decision to return to Riverbend, this moment told her she'd made the right choice. She loved her sister and her brothers, and she wouldn't have missed this for the world.

"Come on." Grace tugged Lucy by the hand. "Anna and Kyle want us in there."

Lucy turned to Hal. She hated to leave him behind but had no idea what Kyle would say to Hal walking in while his wife was giving birth.

Hal's gaze held understanding. "I'll be right here."

"Oh, you don't have to stay," Lucy said quickly.

"Yes, I do."

His quiet assuredness made Lucy's heart turn over. When she'd first left home years ago, she'd preferred men with tailored suits and snappy comebacks, charmers who complimented her left and right.

She was glad to throw all that away for Hal's hint of smile, warm eyes, and the way he said without words that he'd always be waiting for her.

———

HAL SPENT THE NEXT FEW HOURS IN THE COURTYARD where cell signals worked making phone calls. He knew he technically didn't need to remain at the clinic—Lucy would want to be with her family, and Ray would get Lucy home safely if she went to her house at all.

But something made him linger. This was a special time in Lucy's life, and Hal didn't want to walk away from it.

The look in her eyes when she'd said she'd be devastated if something happened to him had struck him hard. Hal wanted to hang onto that, to be there for anything she might need.

Meanwhile, he touched base with his old friends and contacts in the rodeo world, some of whom had become bull wranglers like himself. He even put a call into Gerard Jefferson, who was so famous now that a PA answered for him and vaguely promised to relay the message.

Hal didn't find a lot of answers, but his friends agreed to keep watch for the Redferns, and for anyone who might hold a grudge against them and Hal.

After a couple of hours of talking and then Hal pacing upstairs in the waiting area, Kyle bounced out of the maternity ward, radiating happiness.

"Lucy said you were here." Kyle made a wide gesture to the door. "Get the hell in there."

Hal backed up a step. "I don't want to intrude on your day, Malory."

"Don't be stupid. Come on and see my kid."

The baby was here then. Hal, interested and grateful, followed a buoyant Kyle back into the ward.

Several families from around the county were having

babies today too. The halls were full smiling, excited dads and proud new grandparents.

Lucy came out to meet them, her eyes shining. She took Hal by the hand and led him into Anna's room after Kyle.

Grace was there with Faith, who both greeted Hal eagerly. Ray stood quietly in a corner, watching the tableau. His wife, Drew, whose belly showed she'd be doing this in a few months herself, stood next to him, while her daughter, Erica, bounced with pre-teen energy.

Dr. Anna lay in a bed, exhausted but happy, a tiny bundle in her arms. Hal stepped closer when Lucy led him forward, and he looked down into a scrunched red face.

"This is Tina," Anna said softly. "Our daughter."

"Hey, Tina." Hal bent to her, afraid to touch something so small with his giant fingers. "Welcome."

Lucy's hand tightened on his. Hal glanced at her and found both joy and longing in her expression.

Did Lucy want children? It wasn't a given that all women did—kids were a huge stress and responsibility. A lot of love went into it, sure, but Hal had seen too many kids messed up to believe that all families lived in a reservoir of happiness. His own youth had been spent in mindless contentment that he didn't even realize until he was older, but that didn't happen for everyone.

Of course, if Lucy *did* want kids ... His imagination leapt forward to Lucy smiling down at a little boy or little girl who looked a lot like her.

He suppressed the thought. *I am seriously jumping the gun.* They hadn't even had a real date yet.

"I won the pool," Lucy said with triumph. "I decided you were smart to put your money on a girl, but I came the closest in weight: eight pounds, two ounces. I said eight pounds, one."

"Yeah, you and your number smarts," Kyle said. He pushed past Hal and Lucy to kiss Anna, the love between them engulfing mom, dad, and daughter. It was clear he didn't give a damn about the bets.

Hal basked in the warmth of the Malory family as they drew together to welcome this new life. They'd included him in their gatherings before, but this one brought home to him that he'd been alone for a long time. Hadn't realized until now just how alone.

Lucy held his hand like she was throwing him a lifeline. He clung to it, happy he had her to save him from drowning.

———

HAL TOOK HIS LEAVE WHEN THE MALORY'S MOM, DIANE, arrived with her boyfriend to see her new granddaughter, figuring it was time to let the family be together. He murmured a good-bye into Lucy's ear and left as she surged forward to hug her mother.

Ray walked out with him. The sun was high as they exited through the clinic's doors, the day turning hot, as it could in early spring. Wind blew across the fields, bending grasses and bluebonnets and wafting earthy scents to them.

"Congratulations on your niece," Hal said as they moved through the half-empty parking lot. "Not long from now, that will be you in there, in a panic."

"True," Ray admitted.

They reached Hal's truck, in which Kyle had been hyperventilating a few short hours ago. Hal had told him that by no means could he throw up on the floorboards.

"Are you escorting me outside to tell me to respect your

sister?" Hal asked as Ray lingered. "No need, as I told you before. I respect the hell out of her."

"Maybe, but things are getting serious." Ray met Hal's gaze. "Very serious."

"I know she's recovering from a lot of pain," Hal said, speaking slowly but succinctly. "I get that. Like I told you and Kyle at the diner, I'll never hurt her, I promise you. If she doesn't want anything more to do with me, she's free to dump me. I'll leave it up to her."

Ray regarded him a while longer. "Lucy might not know what she wants to do. That bastard really tore her up inside, and I only now see her recovering—being more like her old self. I don't want to watch that go away again."

"Neither do I." Hal hesitated, then decided to speak his heart. "I love her, Ray. All right?"

Ray's eyes narrowed. "You sure about that?"

"Damn sure. But hey, I'm not going to pressure her, rush her, push her, nothing like that. She has no obligation to feel the same way about me."

Ray stood in silence for a time. Even only a year ago, Ray might have pinned Hal against his truck and threatened him with bodily harm if he upset Lucy in any way. Today, Ray blinked and cleared his throat.

"I've heard about the guys who might be after you," Ray said. "Keep Lucy out of the crossfire, do you hear me?"

"I've been trying to do that since Redfern turned up in town," Hal told him. "The last thing I want is for Lucy to be in danger."

"No, the last thing you want is what Kyle and me will do to you if something happens to her." Ray's gaze went flinty as Hal started to smile. "What's funny?"

"Nothing." Hal forced his lips to flatten out. "I was

thinking you're being way nicer to me than you'd have been before you met Drew."

The mention of Drew made Ray relax. "She's changed me, that's true." The glitter returned to his eyes. "Doesn't mean Kyle and I won't kick your ass."

"I know." Hal stuck out his hand. "Congratulations on the latest Malory. When little Tina grows up to be a beautiful Malory lady, you can threaten all *her* boyfriends."

Ray's determination returned. "I'll do that."

"I probably will too."

Ray clasped Hal's offered hand with a grip that told Hal he meant everything he'd said. Hal nodded, acknowledging.

The two men parted, Ray to return to his welcoming family, Hal to his lonely, workaholic life, and the troubles that threatened to take away the contentedness he'd finally found.

———

BEAUTIFUL DAY FOR THE RODEO, LUCY THOUGHT. SHE SAT in the stands with Christina and Jess, who'd come to watch Grant and Tyler do some exhibition stunt riding. Lucy was there to see Hal round up bulls after they bucked off their riders, a job more dangerous than people realized.

The next event began, featuring bull riders who were competing for the championship today, which would give them points toward the grand prizes at the end of the season.

The voice of Clint, Riverbend's MC and self-professed comedian, blasted over the loudspeaker. "One rider had to scratch in this round, folks. Kyle Malory, who just became a new dad!"

The crowd let out a collective "Awwww!" followed by some cheering. Below Lucy, four young women whose ample busts filled out shirts that stated *We love Kyle Malory* clung to each other for support.

"I'd have let him be *my* baby daddy," one said with tears in her voice.

Lucy rolled her eyes, and Christina laughed at her. "If you marry a handsome cowboy, you have to get used to the buckle bunnies," she said. Jess, on her other side, nodded in agreement.

Lucy knew that neither Grant nor Tyler had eyes for any other women than their wives. They were lucky ladies.

She searched for Hal and spotted him in the arena, waiting by the rail while the first rider prepared himself in the chute. Hal wore a red, white, and blue vertically striped shirt and baggy jeans, and had painted his face with white streaks on his cheeks and red on the tip of his nose. In all this garb, he still managed to be a sexy hunk.

Some rodeo clowns were there to entertain—one heckled Clint from the ring and made the crowd laugh. But most were bullfighters who would wrangle loose bulls, distract them from injured riders, and make sure everyone stayed safe.

Hal had given up the glory of competing to help riders instead. That fact warmed Lucy to her toes.

The first competitor left the chute, the brown-and-white bull he was on bucking hard. The crowd started yelling their support as the clock, which Lucy knew could seem very slow to the rider, ticked away the seconds.

Hal and the second bullfighting clown in the ring followed the action at a safe distance, dodging behind the red plastic barrels they used to protect themselves from the bull's horns and hooves.

The rider was on the ground after four seconds, the bull twisting and dancing away in his freedom. Immediately, Hal and the second clown darted out to distract the animal while the cowboy limped to a gate.

Hal and his partner drove the bull back to a chute, where others waited to pen it. The crowd cheered for them as Hal returned to his barrel to await the next rider.

Lucy tingled with anticipation about seeing him tonight. Even if they simply went to the diner or for a walk, she didn't mind. She only wanted to be with him.

Hal had been elusive since Tina's arrival. Lucy at first assumed he was giving her time to be aunty to her new niece, but Ray had negated this idea. According to Ray, Hal was working with Ross to clear the bad guys out of town. Ray figured Hal would call Lucy once the problem had been resolved.

Hal hadn't canceled the date with Lucy, so she continued to hold the assumption that it was going ahead. *She* was showing up for it anyway, even if she had to arrive on Hal's doorstep and demand him to come with her. Ray had been trying to discourage her from going anywhere at all, but she'd ceased obeying her older brothers when she'd been all of two years old.

The event continued, Hal running agilely to round up the bulls without getting gored by them. His companion entertained the crowd by doing backflips when nothing was going on, but Hal would only patiently wait by the gate for the next rider to appear.

Once that competition had finished, a cowboy from Luckenbach winning the round, the ring cleared. The rodeo clowns took a much-deserved rest, while Grant and Tyler entered to do some trick riding.

Tyler rode in standing on his galloping horse's back, then he dropped down to race his horse around and around the ring.

Grant faced backward on his saddle, then whipped forward then backward again, waving his hat at the spectators as his horse galloped in a circle, perfectly intersecting with Tyler and his mount.

Christina and Jess whooped for the loves of their lives, and the audience yelled their appreciation. Lucy absently cheered Grant's and Tyler's antics as she scanned the milling crowd outside the ring for Hal.

She didn't see him. She did spy Deputies Sanchez and Harrison as well as a couple of uniformed cops, roaming through the milling riders. Ross's orders, no doubt.

As Lucy craned to continue her search, her line of sight was momentarily blocked by Manny Judd, who climbed up the bleachers to drop into the seat beside her.

"There," Manny said, pointing. Lucy followed his finger to a knot of men in cowboy hats who were standing silently together in the backstage area. They weren't watching Grant and Tyler but scrutinizing the waiting bull riders as though searching for someone.

"Those are the guys I saw at the music fest," Manny declared. "They're after Hal, I just know it."

CHAPTER EIGHTEEN

Hal leaned against a corral railing far from the main ring, taking a breather while Grant and Tyler performed. He welcomed the time to rest his limbs before he had to chase down more bovines. One bull had gone for him already, horns in position to send Hal flying, but Hal's experience let him evade the collision.

Dr. Anna had been an awesome wrangler when she'd done her stint as a rodeo clown. The bulls calmed down for her, some walking out docilely behind her to the joy of the crowd. She had a way with animals, that was certain.

Lucy had said she'd be busier than ever now that Dr. Anna would be home for a time, which was probably just as well. Not only did he want Lucy far from him if anyone came after him, but if Hal saw Lucy more often, he might get used to it. His heart would be sliced up all the worse if things didn't work out.

It was all up in the air at the moment, as he would have been if that bull had reached him.

"Hal!" Lucy's voice came to him like music.

Hal swung around to see Lucy jogging toward him, the lanky Manny in her wake.

She was delectable in tight jeans and a chest-hugging button-down shirt. Boots protected her from mud and cow shit, and a straw cowboy hat covered her curls. She was a sight for sore eyes in this crowd of mud-spattered cowboys, burly rodeo clowns, and pissed-off bulls.

"Hal, they're here," Lucy announced.

Hal tore his focus from Lucy's beauty, coming alert. "Who are?"

"The guys who might be after you," Manny said. "I saw them. They're over there."

Manny pointed through crowds of riders, managers, wranglers, and others around the back corrals. His sweeping gesture could have been directed at anyone, but Hal realized he meant the four men who were scanning the area instead of watching Tyler's and Grant's show. They didn't quite fit in—they weren't interested in the riding, nor did they wear the tense anticipation of the competitors. These four were watchful, intent, and looking around with purpose.

"Manny, go find Deputy Sanchez," Hal said, keeping his gaze on the four men. Ross had provided extra security, as promised, but Ross's guys could only cover so much ground. "Lucy, you go home."

Manny, understanding the danger, took off, his long legs propelling him quickly toward the arena.

"Excuse me?" Lucy's eyes went wide. "I refuse to let those assholes ruin my day for me. *You* should go. Ross will arrest them. End of problem."

Arguing would take too much time. Hal grasped Lucy by the arm, and propelled her ahead of him toward the parking lot.

"I'm only going if you come with me," Lucy warned.

Hal didn't answer. The parking area was plenty busy. People came and went to the two-day rodeo or hung out on the fringes with their friends and family, waiting for whatever event they'd made the trip to see. Food trucks were doing good business on the periphery, with people lining up for tacos or ice cream.

Hal spied Lucy's small car in the middle of the morass and steered her in that direction.

Lucy dug her heels in, proving herself strong. Hal halted to keep from out-and-out dragging her, but he wasn't about to give in.

"Look." Lucy jerked her chin at the four men who'd drifted behind them into the parking lot.

They weren't hurrying to chase down Hal, nor even seemed to have noticed him. They'd paused to surround a tall, lean man with gray hair and a perpetual scowl.

"Is that Nate's dad?" Lucy asked. Lucy hadn't met the man, but the resemblance between father and son was clear. Same arrogant stance, same stubborn set of shoulders. "Crap, are they going to attack *him* now?"

That's what it looked like. Hal dimly wondered why Kent Redfern was still in Riverbend—maybe he hadn't taken Nate far after all.

Hal wasn't fond of Kent, but four bullies assaulting a sixty-year-old man wasn't what he wanted to see. He guided Lucy toward her car again.

"Please go home," he said when they reached it. "Or at least somewhere not here. I bet Dr. Anna would love a visit from you."

Lucy rolled her eyes, but she stayed put while Hal left her to head for the clump of men.

He increased his speed as he neared them, worried they'd start in on Kent before he could reach them. He hoped Manny had found Sanchez by now, and that Ross would send his men to converge on these guys with all force.

The ruffians didn't seem to note a large rodeo clown bearing down on them. Kent stood in the middle of the cluster, hands moving while he talked to them. To Hal's relief, they held off their attack for now.

As Hal drew closer, he saw that the gestures Kent made were more like curt commands than those of a scared man begging for his life. The bullyboys were listening, even giving him nods.

Hal slowed, things clicking in his brain. Kent Redfern wasn't afraid of these bastards—he was telling them what to do.

Fuck.

The implications of this hit Hal, stilling his feet. Did this mean that Kent had figured out who'd beaten up Nate and was intimidating the guys with threats of retaliation from his meaner crew?

Or had he ordered them to assault his own son?

Kent didn't seem in any way angry at the moment. He was calm and confident, and the other men gave him their attention without resistance.

Kent lifted his head and gazed straight at Hal. "Nice of you to join us, Jenkins."

The four men jerked around, startled, then they fanned out to flank Hal.

Hal was too stunned to be worried. "Shit, Redfern, did you have these guys take down Nate?"

"I did." Kent acknowledged this with a nod.

Hal recalled Nate's plea before Hal had left him in the

hospital room. *Help me.* Nate had been trying to tell Hal that his own father had ordered a hit on him. Son of a bitch.

"Where the hell have you taken him?" Hal demanded. "Nate wasn't ready to leave the hospital."

"Home." Kent said the word firmly. "Where he belongs." His eyes glittered. "I didn't realize you two were such good friends."

Hal ignored Kent's attempt to goad him. "No one deserves what these guys did to him."

"You don't know shit about it, Jenkins," Kent stated in a hard voice. "Nate ratted out his friends and sent them all to prison, where they're still rotting. He tried to rat *me* out, but I had better lawyers. You don't do that. Not to your friends. Not to your family."

"So having these dudes kick his ass was your answer?" Hal asked in amazement.

Kent pressed his mouth into a thin line. "Yes, and they're going to kick yours too. You're as much to blame for the arrests as Nate. You don't do that." He repeated the words, his eyes as hard as steel balls.

Hal wasn't exactly ready for a fight right now. He was in his clown getup, which was great for running around rings, but his loose shirt and suspenders might give his opponents handholds.

On the other hand, he'd put together the outfit for major maneuverability. Bulls were even more dangerous than these losers.

Kent obviously wasn't giving Hal a choice. The four men converged around him with cold intent. One held a length of rebar in his gloved hands.

They went for him. Two hung back, probably thinking

their friends, especially the one with the rebar, could easily take down a lone man in clown makeup.

Hal made them doubt their wisdom. He jammed his fist in the first man's face and swung to elbow the gut of the second. At the same time, Hal grabbed the second man's wrist and twisted it, forcing him to release the rebar.

The rebar hit the dirt, but more fists came at Hal as the other two joined in. Hal's right leg buckled when a kick landed on it, but he caught himself and spun away, experience making him agile.

Two of the guys circled behind him, and the rebar wielder retrieved his weapon. Hal wasn't getting out of this any time soon.

Kent stood a few paces behind his bullyboys, watching the fight dispassionately. He was waiting calmly for them to take Hal out—either to punish him or to kill him, Hal wasn't sure.

He would do his damnedest to stay alive, but it was going to take some hard work.

I love you, Luce, Hal sent out into the universe, then he swung to face the men surging on him.

Fists flew, Hal getting in many good punches and jabs while avoiding the rebar that hurtled toward him. He ducked and hit, spun and elbowed. He felt a sting as the skin on his face opened, but in the thick of battle, he barely noted it.

One of the fighters kicked Hal in the back of his knee, and this time, he went down. Hal rolled so he wouldn't land flat on his face, striking out as he went.

Black-gloved fingers tapped the shoulder of one of the men. Hal watched in dim comprehension as the guy spun around to face a grinning Tyler Campbell.

Tyler's fist caught the man between the eyes. The man

grunted but didn't fall. He lunged at Tyler, who glided lithely out of the way, nimble from a lifetime of stunt riding.

A larger set of hands pulled a man off Hal just as a fist was about to connect with Hal's face. Ray Malory, minus Tyler's merry smile, lifted the assailant high into the air, the man's legs flailing. Ray dropped the guy and landed a swift blow to his jaw, sending him to the ground.

Ray sidestepped the fallen man and reached down to lift Hal to his feet.

It was good to have someone as big as Ray at his back. The two of them faced Kent's remaining hired bullies, who were shaking off the punches and ready to fight again. Tyler glee-fully continued to engage the one he'd intercepted, with Grant leaping in to assist.

Then Jack Hillman was running at them, his hard-as-hell eyes making the assailants falter. Jack evaded the man who slashed at him with the rebar, grabbed the guy's arm, and broke it.

The rebar hit the ground a second time, the fighter who'd held it howling in pain. Jack stepped aside and the man limped away, holding his arm.

He didn't get far. Deputy Sanchez, who grinned as much as Tyler, had the guy cuffed in two seconds flat.

Adam and Carter next came out of the crowd. Behind them were Manny, who jumped up and down, yelling his encouragement, and Lucy, worried but determined.

The remaining bullies took one look at Carter, recognized a man who'd give them no quarter, and decided to run.

"Grab Kent," Hal yelled at the Campbells, blood spraying from his sliced lip. "He instigated all this."

Kent, the moment law enforcement had shown up, had

quietly turned on his heel and began striding for the parking
lot.

Carter and Adam immediately started after him, but Ross,
who seemed to appear out of nowhere in his uniform, beat
them to it.

"Kent Redfern," Ross announced. "I'm arresting you for
the assault of Nate Redfern and Hal Jenkins, and for the
conspiracy to commit assault."

Kent pretended shock, as though Ross had to be mistaken,
then he tried to run. Adam and Carter were on him before he
could take two steps. A moment after that, Ross clicked cuffs
around Kent's wrists.

Jack, Tyler, Grant, Ray, and Sanchez surrounded the
remaining members of Kent's crew, who'd decided to surrender. Manny kept darting forward, as though he'd join in, and
then jumped back, aware he'd never last against these guys.

Hal's focus narrowed to Lucy, who stood a little apart from
the others. She'd rounded up the cavalry, he realized. By
fetching the Campbells, Ray, and Jack, Lucy had saved his life.

He started for her.

"Hal," Ross called after him as he began to lead Kent away.
"Go find an EMT and get yourself cleaned up. Then come to
my office to give me your statement."

Hal waved vaguely at him. He must be a mess, with his
clown makeup smeared, and his skin spattered with blood.
One of Hal's eyes smarted, signaling it would soon be black
and blue. He limped, his knee sore from the guy kicking it, but
he couldn't stop himself going to Lucy.

As though a tether pulled him to her, Hal made straight for
her, never noticing anyone in his way. Lucy watched him
come, her lips parting in concern. She didn't move.

Hal reached her. A fierceness settled over her as though

she expected to have to argue with him about why she hadn't tamely gone home.

Without a word, Hal pulled her into his arms. Lucy started, her straw hat falling to the dirt, but soon her embrace encompassed him, infusing him with new strength. Hal kissed her fragrant hair, everything bad going away.

Lucy eased from him but only to cup his cheek. "Oh, Hal. You okay?"

Hal couldn't answer. He scooped her to him and responded with a hard kiss on her mouth.

His cut lip hurt like hell, but Hal didn't care. He sensed Ray, the Campbells, and Jack eyeing them intently, and he still didn't care. Hal kissed Lucy with yearning, letting his body meld to hers, her touch healing his battered heart.

Hal ended the kiss to find Lucy gazing at him with soft eyes, her compassion shutting out the harshness of the rest of the world.

He brushed back Lucy's hair with gentle fingers and kissed her forehead. "Thank you, love," Hal whispered. "Thank you for rescuing me."

CHAPTER NINETEEN

Lucy did not see Hal much for the next week. He hadn't wanted to cancel their date Saturday night after the rodeo, but Lucy insisted he go home and rest after a trip to the ER to make sure he was all right.

Rest *alone*, Lucy had emphasized. Lucy knew what would happen if she accompanied him home to nurse him. She'd never keep her hands off him, and Hal probably wouldn't push her away.

But Lucy worried about him. He'd taken a beating and needed to heal.

Lucy felt virtuous for letting him mend, but she chafed to see him. However, she'd been correct that she'd be very busy once Anna became a mom. Dr. Calvert, the small-statured but robust vet from Llano, was friendly enough and easy to work with, but Lucy had a lot on her plate showing him what was where and introducing him to Anna's clients.

Dr. Calvert also took over the Wednesday appointment at Callie's ranch, and this week was especially busy. Callie had brought in three new horses, two of which had colds, and they had to be isolated and treated, plus all the humans had to constantly wash up and even change clothes to keep from spreading the disease to the other horses.

Hal phoned Lucy every day, keeping her up to date on his progress. He was strong, and he assured her that he healed fast. He set another date for them the following Saturday afternoon.

Why the afternoon, Hal wouldn't tell her. Lucy would have to wait and see, he said.

"I'm not sure I like surprises," she'd growled at him. "I have an overactive imagination."

Hal, the shit, only laughed, said good-bye, and hung up.

Kent Redfern and his four henchmen had been arrested. His bullies all had warrants for crimes in their past, plus Kent's part in the doping ring in San Angelo was being reinvestigated. He'd never been tried for it, according to Ross, but Ross predicted he'd not be able to avoid it this time.

Lucy thought she'd never forget the heart-stopping moment when she'd realized that Nate's father was the leader of the gang instead of its victim. The four men had come at Hal, and Lucy had run as fast as her booted feet would carry her to Tyler and Grant, just exiting the ring after their performance, babbling that Hal was in trouble.

Both men had enthusiastically rushed to his defense. Lucy had called Ross, fingers shaking, to make certain he knew what was going on. Grimly, he'd said he had received word from Sanchez, and he and his men were heading that way.

Then Adam and Carter, who'd wondered why their brothers had raced from the stunt show, saw what was going on and also ran to help. Jack, who'd happened by, stopped for Lucy to explain, then with a steely determination, joined the fray. Manny had come along with Deputy Sanchez and some uniforms about that time, completing the team.

Kent had tried to claim that he and his crew were innocent bystanders attacked by Hal and his friends, but Lucy had been a witness to the entire event and declared she'd stand up and report everything in court.

Ross had taken Lucy's statement at his office but told her the odds of her having to appear as a witness were slim. The guys Kent had hired had done worse in their pasts, and they'd likely be convicted on those crimes first. Kent, of course, would lawyer up, as he had before. However, he'd confessed to Hal that he'd ordered the attack on Nate, and Kent's crew would probably flip on him.

Hal apparently had called everyone in southwest Texas in the past week and recruited them to look for Nate, who had been found in a cheap motel halfway between Riverbend and San Angelo. He'd been left in bed there in much pain, and Hal's friends had taken Nate to a hospital in San Angelo for treatment. They'd also arranged a safer place for him to stay once he was discharged, to wait and see what would happen with Kent.

"Nate's pretending not to be grateful," Hal had told Lucy on the phone. "He says he's pissed off at me for interfering— that he asked for my help only because he was messed up on medication. But Nate also knows how dangerous his dad is, and my friends say he's relieved to be away from him."

"I didn't like Nate," Lucy said. "I'm still mad at him for everything he did to you. But abusive parents are horrible. His dad really screwed up his life."

"Nate said that coming here looking for me was part of his plan to make his dad proud of him," Hal said. "He thought he'd force me to help him restart his business and gain praise from his old man. But Kent is a piece of work. He was punishing Nate for not only getting most of their old crew lengthy prison sentences, but for seeking me out once he was ready to roll again. Kent never trusted me—with good reason, it's true. I remember Nate always trying to please his dad, and never being able to. Nate's thirty-five and still trying to show his father he's capable."

"That's just sad," Lucy said.

"It is." Hal let out a sigh. "I hope Nate learns to live without the man, no matter what happens."

"I do too."

They'd shared a moment of silent sympathy for Nate, then Hal cleared his throat. "Are we still on for Saturday? I'll pick you up at your house around three, all right?"

"Sounds good. What's the dress code?"

"Hmm?" Hal sounded distracted. "Oh. Anything you want."

"Never tell a woman that. I might show up in a chiffon evening gown and heels. Or sloppy shorts and a tank top."

Hal chuckled. "You'll be beautiful no matter what you wear. But, you know. Ordinary clothes."

"You are such a guy." Lucy laughed, though she heated all over at his calling her beautiful.

They finished the call, but exchanged no endearments as they hung up. Was their relationship at that point yet? Lucy wondered. Did they even have a relationship? She supposed they did, but she had no idea how to define it.

Lucy was off Saturday, so she had all morning to fret about that afternoon's date. Was Hal whisking her to a romantic B&B? If so, would he let her pack? Or would he take her horse-back riding in the countryside? That meant boots and sturdy jeans. Or were they going into Fredericksburg to have tea in one of its charming restaurants?

She tried to picture Hal sipping tea from a dainty cup, quirking his pinky, and gave up.

Lucy finally decided on jeans with a nice blouse and gray leather boots that could look good in a casual restaurant as well as be practical for horseback riding.

Restless after that, she drifted to the front porch to wait. The day was sunny but cooler, with a brisk breeze. A light jacket was enough to cut the wind while Lucy lounged against her porch railing, trying not to glare too impatiently down the street.

"Are you going out, honey?" Mrs. Kaye called from her garden next door.

"Yes. With Hal." Lucy straightened up, resting her hands on the porch railing. Her eyes narrowed. "You started the rumor that we were sleeping together, didn't you?"

Mrs. Kaye blinked, an expression of innocence on her face. "What are you talking about, dear?"

"It *was* you," Lucy said with conviction. "You heard that Hal refused tell anyone where he'd been that night. You knew he never beat up Nate, and you wanted Ross to leave him alone. You figured right that he'd be embarrassed if you let on he'd been on your porch watching my house. But you also knew everyone would believe it if you claimed he'd been with me that night."

Mrs. Kaye gazed at her in bewilderment a moment longer, then she dropped the act and sent Lucy a sly wink. "Worked, didn't it?"

"At the expense of my reputation," Lucy pointed out.

Mrs. Kaye spluttered a laugh. "Spare me your protests, young lady. You were perfectly happy to have the world believe you and Hal were an item, because you hated how everyone felt sorry for you. Lucy Malory does not want to be an object of pity. Now, you aren't. You've shaken off your past and moved on in the eyes of the world. Well, in the eyes of River County, anyway."

Every word Mrs. Kaye spoke was true. Lucy wasn't angry at her, hadn't really been even when she'd realized that Mrs. Kaye had to have been the one who spread the story.

"Just so you know, it's not a rumor anymore," Lucy said, her cheeks warming.

"I didn't think it was, dear." Mrs. Kaye sent her a look of understanding. "You two have actually been together since you came home, you know. I'm glad you've both finally faced that. Oh, here comes Hal now."

Hal's large pickup made its slow way up the empty street to halt in front of the short walkway to Lucy's house. Hal hopped out and went around the front of the truck to open the door for Lucy.

"Hey, Mrs. Kaye," Hal tipped his cowboy hat to her on the way.

"Hey yourself, Hal." Mrs. Kaye beamed at him. "You two be happy now, you hear?"

Hal nodded at her then sent Lucy a baffled look when he joined her in the truck. Lucy chuckled.

"Mrs. Kaye loves to manipulate everyone into doing exactly what she wants and then pretends she never did a thing." She buckled her seatbelt as Hal pulled from the curb. "I hear she was a wild thing in her younger years."

"Yeah, I heard that too."

"She's showed me photos," Lucy said. "She and her friends with long hair and miniskirts, holding up beers, sometimes flipping off the camera. I loved it."

Hal laughed with her then drove around Riverbend's town square and out to the main highway.

"Any hint as to where we're going?" Lucy asked. "You wouldn't believe what I have in my purse just in case."

"In case what?" Hal asked curiously.

"In case we end up at a B&B or on a flight to Tahiti. But if it's Tahiti, I'll need a bathing suit. Sunscreen. A cute dress."

"Not going anywhere that far," Hal said in amusement. "Not far at all, in fact."

He abruptly turned off the highway onto a road that led to a handful of houses placed in the folds of pleasant hills. They were fairly close to the Malory ranch, which was, in fact, on the other side of one of these hills.

"Visiting friends?" Lucy guessed. "Or fossil hunting? I should have brought a trowel. Oh, wait, I know. You said you're thinking about house shopping."

From the slight dismay on Hal's face, Lucy knew her last guess was the correct one.

"Really?" Lucy went on with eager interest. "One of these houses? They're so nice. I didn't know any were for sale."

Hal parked his truck in front of one of the larger homes— two-story with cupolas, a bay window on the ground floor, and a wraparound porch. The siding was painted a creamy yellow, the porch trim dark blue with a red highlight here and there. The large yard had a trimmed lawn in front but a natural meadow full of spring flowers surrounding the house's other sides. Live oak trees were dotted about to provide shade but not block the view.

Hal once again strode around the truck to hold the door for Lucy before she could descend. He would always do that, she realized.

"It's beautiful." Lucy stepped from the pickup and gazed

admiringly at the house. "But ..." She waved her hand at the strip of yard that lined the road. "No *For Sale* sign. Is this a wish-list house?"

Hal shook his head. "The man who owns it is a friend of Kennedy's who's going to sell up and move to the Gulf Coast. I said I was looking, and Kennedy spoke to him. The owner said he'd let me give him the first offer."

"And did you?"

"Yep." Hal slid off his hat. "And he accepted."

"Well, congratulations." Lucy eyed the house with envy. She liked the little place she rented, but it was tiny, and she couldn't do much with it. "You'll certainly have plenty of room here. Can I give you tips from time to time on how to decorate? I promise not to interfere too much."

"I want you to." Hal rested his hat against his blue-jeaned thigh. "In fact, I was hoping you'd live here with me."

Lucy had drawn a breath to continue reasons why she should help him, but the breath froze halfway in. Only a quiet squeak escaped her throat.

"You okay?" Hal asked in alarm.

Lucy coughed. "You ... *What?*"

"I said I was hoping you'd live here with me." Hal's repeated words held less optimism. "It's okay if you don't want to."

"Of course, I want to." Lucy's reply tumbled out, louder than she meant. "You stunned me, that's all. Is this your surprise? Then this is a *good* surprise. I never dreamed you were going to show me *this*."

Hal's smile was full of relief. "You like it?"

"Like it?" Lucy swung to him. "I love it! It's beautiful. I'd love to live here with you, Hal. Damn the expense."

She'd find some way to make it work. That was how Lucy

rolled with her life—she jumped in with both feet and then worked like hell to enjoy the swim. She'd always thrived like that—except for the whole Clyde debacle, of course.

Clyde was long ago and far away now, and Lucy's time with him had rapidly faded from her memory.

None of her past life mattered anymore. *This* was important—Lucy standing in front of a beautiful house in Riverbend, close to home and family, with a hot cowboy with a heart of gold at her side.

"I have plenty put by," Hal said. "Neither of us will have to work our fingers to the bone to keep it up. Plus, I'm selling my little house—you'd be surprised how much people will pay for places like that these days."

He'd thought this through, Lucy realized. Much more practical than her impulsive reaction.

"Are you sure you want to do this?" Lucy made herself ask. "It's a lot to take on."

"Very sure. I want to live here, and I want to live here with you." Hal turned to her, his hand going tenderly to her cheek. "I love you."

Lucy's body trembled as all the hurts and pains of her past drained from her and fled. Release. She was here in the sunshine and cool breeze with Hal, the man of her heart.

"I love *you*," Lucy said softly. "I should have told you that before." She rested her hands on his chest, feeling the strength of him. "You've been here for me from the moment I arrived back in Riverbend. Protecting me. Listening to me, really hearing me. I've loved you for a long time."

A flush stole over Hal's hard face. "Well, that's good to know."

Lucy rose on tiptoes and gently kissed his mouth, never mind who might be watching from the house.

Hal tugged her against him. His answering kiss was full of promise, not only of love but of passion so hot it already singed her. Too bad the house wasn't theirs already—they could run inside and break it in, in the best way. Though they could always go back to her place right now. Or his.

Lucy laughed quietly when the kiss finished. "If we buy a house together, that blows our Tahiti trip."

"Not necessarily." Hal dropped his hat to the pavement. "It might make a good honeymoon."

"Honeymoon." Lucy repeated the word then watched in bewilderment as Hal lowered himself to land on one knee before her.

"Yep." Hal cleared his throat. "If you'll marry me, that is."

Lucy gaped at him, her breath deserting her once more. Hal watched her in some anxiety, as though thinking he'd maybe gone too far.

"If I'll marry you?" Lucy wet her dry lips, every limb shaking. She opened her mouth to yell, *Yes*, but again, only a tiny squeak emerged.

Hal started to rise, dejected, but Lucy shoved him back down then fell to her knees with him.

"You big sweetie." Lucy gulped breaths, then declared loudly, for the sky and trees and all the neighbors to hear, "I *will* marry you, Hal Jenkins. I can't think of a thing that would make me happier."

Hal relaxed. "That's good. That's very good."

Lucy knelt in the join of his thighs, need boiling through her as Hal kissed her again. The kiss held joy, relief, possession, and the sexiness that only Hal could bring.

They kissed there in the sunshine, bluebonnets nodding their encouragement, as the Texas breeze touched them and took their soft laughter to the vivid blue sky.

EPILOGUE

The Bluebonnet Festival at Ray and Drew Malory's B&B wasn't really Jack's thing, but he showed up like a good friend.

He had to admit that the fields, blue-violet with flowers, were pretty against the green hills and towering trees. Also, Ray and Drew knew how to throw a party.

Jack procured himself a beer, inwardly amused at the children who broke their wild games of chase to eye him in both curiosity and trepidation. He found himself shade under a big tree, happy to cool off. Yesterday, it had been freezing, literally. Today, it was in the high 80s. A Texas spring at its most unpredictable.

The whole town must be here. Ray and Drew with their daughter, Erica, greeted their guests and made sure they had plenty of food and drink. Dr. Anna sat on the porch, her two-week-old daughter in her arms. Every single person had to stop by to see the new baby and congratulate Anna. Anna would be exhausted by the end of the day if she wasn't already.

Campbells filled the spaces—the five brothers, their wives,

and their growing brood. Those boys could reproduce. The Malorys were proving they weren't far behind.

Lucy Malory, dark curls dancing, hopped up on the porch in the middle of the tumult, grabbed a metal bar, and clanged the old-fashioned triangle that hung above her.

"What is she doing?" Jack muttered to himself. There was no formal dinner to summon anyone to—this was a cookout, and already going strong.

"I think she has something to say." Karen materialized from behind him, moving to stand very close to Jack.

With her smooth scent and welcome warmth next to him, Jack abruptly didn't give a shit what Lucy was up to. He hadn't seen Karen in a couple of weeks, as their respective businesses had kept them jumping.

Jack took a chance and slid his arm around Karen's waist. She sent him a smile and didn't pull away.

Lucy raised her hands. "Friends, family, various guests of the B&B, lend me your ears." A ripple of laughter spread across the lawn as people turned to listen.

Hal climbed to the porch to stand by Lucy in silence. Not many noticed him, their eyes on the vibrant Lucy, but when Hal draped his arm around her, the townspeople began to glance at each other, to murmur.

Ray and Kyle didn't appear to be alarmed. Whatever Lucy was going to share, they weren't worried.

"Hal wants to tell y'all something," Lucy said.

She and Hal must have rehearsed this because Hal didn't look like he wanted to turn and flee. He remained beside Lucy, waiting until everyone quieted enough to listen.

"Lucy and me," Hal began. "We're engaged."

A stunned silence fell. Then Manny Judd let out a yowl of joy, leaping into the air as he liked to do. By the time he came down, the entire party was cheering. Jack swore he could see Hal's blush from this distance, but the man stared at the crowd defiantly, firmly locked to Lucy's side.

Lucy was radiant with joy. She shrieked playfully as friends and family rushed to her to embrace, kiss, and congratulate.

Ray and Kyle clicked beer bottles together in satisfaction. Obviously, they'd known about the engagement and were happy with it. Otherwise, they'd be shitting bricks.

"Good for them." Karen had clapped in her urbane way, then she dropped her poise and let out a shrill whistle through her fingers. "Mrs. Kaye," Karen yelled, waving at the demure woman. "I won!"

Mrs. Kaye, at a picnic table with the librarian and other friends, waved back happily.

"You won what?" Jack asked.

Karen slipped her hand to the crook of Jack's arm. "The betting pool. Mrs. Kaye had one going about Hal and Lucy. I wagered we'd hear of their engagement by the Bluebonnet Festival. I just won a decent amount of cash." She glanced up at Hal, her eyes unreadable. "Maybe we could go to a nice place I know in Galveston."

Jack's heart skipped a beat. He and Karen hadn't had more than stolen moments, a night here, a drink at the bar there. They'd never gone away together.

"That might be good," Jack said.

Karen watched him as though she wasn't certain he was being polite or truly wanted to go.

"All right then," she said. "I'll set it up."

Jack kept his eye on the crowd, which had gone back to eating, drinking, laughing, and conversing at the tops of their voices.

"I wonder if Mrs. Kaye has a bet going about us," Jack remarked.

He felt Karen's start. "She might. I wonder what the odds are?" She spoke lightly, without looking at him.

Jack tugged her close again. "I think we should let them keep guessing."

Karen turned her gaze to him now, her soft laughter moving her wonderfully against him. "Maybe we should."

Jack would have to guess himself. Whenever he was with Karen, he felt more relaxed than any other time. Contented almost, though he'd never tell her that. And in a weird way, complete.

"Things should be pretty quiet in Riverbend right now," Jack observed. Everyone, including Mildred, Ross, and Deputies Sanchez and Harrison, was here.

"Should be," Karen said. "I closed the bar for the day. Told the staff to enjoy themselves."

"Same at my place." Jack knew his employees would rather be here than in the deserted lumberyard and garage.

"I'm guessing the road to my house will be empty," Karen said.

"Could be."

Jack glanced down to find Karen grinning up at him. "I've missed you, Jack."

"Missed you too."

Her eyes widened slightly in surprise at Jack's admission. But he had missed her sharp-witted conversation, the beauty she thought she'd tamed to business-like neatness, and the way she touched him.

Karen's grin became a tight smile. "Shall we go, then?"

"Yep." Jack let himself soften. "I think we shall."

She burst out laughing at his choice of words, her beauty shining out behind the shields she always kept in place.

Before Karen could change her mind, Jack gripped her hand and led her through the trees ringing the makeshift lot toward her sleek car. Their feet moved faster and faster as they let excitement catch them, Karen's laughter winding its way into Jack's heart.

ABOUT THE AUTHOR

New York Times bestselling and award-winning author Jennifer Ashley has more than 100 published novels and novellas in romance, urban fantasy, mystery, and historical fiction under the names Jennifer Ashley, Allyson James, and Ashley Gardner. Jennifer's books have been translated into more than a dozen languages and have earned starred reviews in *Publisher's Weekly* and *Booklist*. When she isn't writing, Jennifer enjoys playing music (guitar, piano, flute), reading, knitting, hiking, and building dollhouse miniatures.

More about Jennifer's books can be found at
http://www.jenniferashley.com

To keep up to date on her new releases, join her newsletter here:
http://eepurl.com/47kLL

Made in the USA
Monee, IL
10 October 2023